FICKLE FORTUNES

*A cozy Scottish mystery
with a great twist*

TRAUDE AILINGER

Published by The Book Folks

London, 2024

ISBN 978-1-80462-211-7

www.thebookfolks.com

Chapter 1

There is someone in everybody's life without whom their existence would be so much more pleasant; that one particular person who provokes even the most cheerful and good-tempered individual into fantasising about murder. Thankfully, most people leave it at that.

By no stretch of the imagination could Detective Inspector Russell McCord ever be called either cheerful or good-tempered, and as he was walking along the corridor towards Superintendent Arthur Gilchrist's office, his mind pictured in grim detail the various ways in which the telegenic features of his superior could be permanently disfigured. By the time he reached the door, visions of disembowelment had taken over, and when the sonorous voice called him in, it took considerable effort to rearrange his face into an expression of mild interest.

"You wanted to see me, sir?"

Gilchrist rose slowly from his leather chair, not out of politeness, McCord was certain, but to enjoy the advantage of being over six-feet tall to his five foot ten inches. McCord, however, despite his poor eating habits, had maintained his slim and sinewy frame by expending his energy relentlessly chasing criminals, while Gilchrist spent most of each day sitting on his broadening bottom.

"I did indeed," Gilchrist said in his plummy accent. "And I'm sure you know why, don't you, McCord?"

As it was the time of year when the assistant chief constable would be reviewing their crime statistics,

McCord had a fair idea of where Gilchrist was going with this, but he was damned if he was going to surrender without a fight.

"I'm not sure I do, sir."

Gilchrist screwed up his face and rubbed his stomach in a deliberate, clockwise motion.

"I am, of course, referring to the Jai Sandhu case," he said accusingly as if McCord was the cause of his digestive problem. "How long have you been working on this?"

Gilchrist knew fine well how long, but McCord answered through clenched teeth. "Sandhu was murdered on 2 March, sir."

"Exactly. Four and a half months ago," Gilchrist said. "And all this time, the killer of a popular member of our Indian community has been roaming the streets and making a mockery of Edinburgh CID."

McCord was sure that the latter worried Gilchrist much more than the former, and he was proved right. Gilchrist stabbed a pile of newspapers that were neatly arranged on his otherwise uncluttered desk.

"Do you know what they call us? Institutionally racist, that's what they call us. And not just the left-wing rags, even the former chief constable says we are. We need to prove them wrong, McCord, and we won't do that by ignoring the murder of an Indian shopkeeper!"

McCord bridled at the injustice of the accusation.

"We haven't ignored the Sandhu case at all, sir," McCord said. "We've investigated all known offenders involved in racially motivated crimes without being able to link any of them to the crime scene. The public appeal didn't bring us a breakthrough either. It seems to have been a random arson attack, which is precisely why it is so difficult to solve. The case is still open, but to be honest, sir, I'm not sure where we can go from here."

"Well, I have done some thinking on your behalf," Gilchrist said, while McCord tried not to roll his eyes. "I've arranged for a film crew from STV to do a re-enactment of the crime, as well as some interviews with members of the public and the police, including myself."

McCord groaned inwardly. That was all he needed; some long-haired media types prancing around the station and getting in the way of real police work. And that would be only the beginning. True-crime programmes invariably led to a sandstorm of crank calls that needed to be sifted through for the one grain of truth that might not be there at all.

Gilchrist looked at McCord with a combination of exasperation and disappointment. "I am well aware of your aversion to public relations, McCord. Nevertheless, I expect your full cooperation. The responsibility of being the face of Edinburgh CID will, of course, fall upon my shoulders. All I want you to do is not annoy the members of the press, and that includes Miss Thornton. Her latest series on the Murrayfield murders was excellent, as usual. Do you think you can do that?"

With a deadpan expression, McCord nodded. Gilchrist scrutinised his face, looking for any sign of insubordination.

"Remember my motto, McCord. 'Hearts and Minds'."

Or, thought McCord, to quote the station's wisecrackers: 'Farts from behind'.

"I do remember," he said and withdrew.

* * *

Back in the Sunset Boulevard, as his office had been unofficially named after being painted a vivid orange colour, McCord was able to vent his frustration in front of DS Duncan Calderwood. In anticipation of his boss's foul mood, Calderwood had fetched decent coffee and a couple of lemon muffins from the café down the road. As soon as McCord spotted them, his face lit up.

"Your expensive education has finally paid off, Calderwood. At long last, you figured out how you can be useful."

Calderwood did not bat an eyelid. "How bad was it?"

"On a scale from one to ten: eleven. Soon the station will be crawling with would-be Spielbergs and extras hoping for an Oscar."

Seeing Calderwood's uncomprehending stare, he added, "Gilchrist is bringing in a TV crew for a re-enactment of the Sandhu case. He's desperate to get it off his crime statistics before the end of the month."

"No pressure then," Calderwood said. "We've only spent the past four months running ourselves ragged and getting nowhere."

"It bugs me, though," McCord said. "To hell with the statistics, but we can't have somebody going round Edinburgh setting fire to corner shops and killing people. Come to think of it, have you checked again if there have been any similar attacks?"

Calderwood shook his head. "The usual vandalism, yes, racially motivated attacks, yes, but nothing with this MO. It's strange, isn't it, that the victim was Sandhu, of all people. You could hardly find anybody more integrated than he was. Leith Academy, Hibs fan; he even stuck a 'yes' poster in his shop window during the independence referendum."

"Racist thugs are not exactly famed for their differentiated thinking," McCord said. "And the obnoxious moron who did this even painted 'Paki go home' on the wall. Sandhu was Indian. Obviously, the arsonist didn't know Sandhu from Adam."

"What's the Super hoping to gain from a TV programme?" Calderwood asked. "All we have is the grainy CCTV footage of someone in dark clothes walking towards the scene and then running away carrying what looks like a petrol canister. How is anybody going to recognise them?"

"They won't," McCord said. "The community officer showed the picture in the whole area round the south end of Leith Walk, but nobody had seen anything."

Calderwood nodded. "I suppose it's possible that somebody was out and about that night, left the area the following day and missed the public appeal."

"Maybe," McCord said, unconvinced. "But I still think it is going to be a criminal waste of time. The only reason we're doing this is to demonstrate that we haven't given up on the case. Maybe instead of the community officer, I'll send Dharwan to speak to the family and the locals. With her language skills and background, she might get something new out of them. If you can spare your girlfriend, that is."

Seeing Calderwood blush, McCord grinned. "Killing two birds with one stone. Dharwan is not only one of our smartest, she also looks gorgeous, and Gilchrist will be really cheesed off if he himself isn't the prettiest face in uniform on the programme." His face lit up. "I know, I'll get you to do some interviews as well, and then Gilchrist will drop to a very poor third place in the beauty stakes."

Calderwood did not take the bait. "I think we should use the opportunity to catch the killer, rather than score points off each other. If the Super wants to put more resources towards the Sandhu case, surely that's a good thing."

McCord regarded his partner with mock admiration. "Not only posh and handsome, but also wise beyond his years." He paused, wondering if he should say something that conveyed how much he liked him, but he quickly rejected that as a silly thought. "Time to clock off," he said instead. "And take Dharwan with you."

"You have a nice evening, too, sir," Calderwood replied with a smile, grabbed his jacket, and left.

McCord was desperate to get home as well, but the thought of crawling through the rush-hour traffic towards Portobello did not appeal. Swinging gently from side to side in his chair, he thought of Amy Thornton and what she might be doing now. Probably walking home from the office of *Forth Write* magazine in George Street.

A dense fog had rolled in from the sea, making it almost dark long before sunset, but her flat was just round the corner in Queen Street, so she should be safe. He wondered if he should call her. Was it too soon, after they had parted only this morning? He smiled as he remembered the time they had spent together on the Isle of May.

Amy had seemed genuinely excited watching the puffins bring in sand eels in their stunningly colourful beaks, and the guillemots and razorbills sitting on their cliff-edge nests. She had laughed at him as he was fumbling with his camera in a panic after he had spotted a barred warbler, but then she supported his arm holding the heavy 500mm lens and even praised the picture he had taken. The storm hadn't yet reached them although a stiff breeze was already tugging at her coat and tousling her dark hair. To his surprise, she had looked happy, and he was happy, too, once the fear had abated that another date might go disastrously wrong.

But just as everything was going swimmingly, storm clouds were beginning to form in the east, and while the day trippers were waiting for their ferry to leave, the skipper was walking to and fro with his mobile clamped to his darkening face. After sitting on damp plastic chairs for almost an hour, they were told that because of the stormy conditions, their ferry had not been cleared to sail and that they would have to spend the night on the island. He had been worried how Amy would take the news, but she declared it an adventure with great potential for an article for the magazine.

They were led to the only large building on the island, the Isle of May Bird Observatory, where, fortunately, there was enough room for the group from the *May Princess* to take shelter. Telling stories of previous trips and countless tales of rare birds they had seen, the group had shared the food that was left over from their picnics; whisky flasks made the rounds, and apart from one guy who kept ranting about the incompetence of the Scottish government, everybody was quite philosophical about their situation, glad to be at least protected from the howling gale and torrential rain outside.

By midnight, when all the food and drink was consumed and all the stories told, it was time to bed down. There were twelve of them but only six mattresses and a pile of blankets, which had caused a brief struggle between survival instinct and altruism, but in the end civility prevailed. Once the two elderly couples had been made comfortable, McCord nabbed one of the remaining mattresses for Amy. He had lain down on the floor next to her, only dozing off in the early hours and sleeping fitfully, making sure that none of the guys there tried any funny business. He was very pleased with himself that he had behaved impeccably, although the memories of him and Amy dancing close at the police charity ball made this very difficult.

In the morning, however, Amy had been in a bad mood, probably because she hadn't slept well either. She had declined his offer of a cooked breakfast at the Anstruther harbour and asked him to take her straight home to get showered and changed for work. But still, she couldn't blame him for the storm, and the whole thing had gone a lot better than their first date, a disastrous outing to a Japanese restaurant. He was spared reliving his utter humiliation of that evening by the ringing of the office phone.

"DI McCord." It was Jack Carruthers, the duty sergeant. "I was wondering if you're still here, sir," he said. "The body of a woman has been found at the bottom of the Crags."

McCord frowned. The Salisbury Crags were a notorious spot for suicides. Tragedies without the thrill of the chase. "Is anybody there securing the scene?"

"Uniforms. SOCOs have been called. The husband found her, apparently, and told them he thinks that she was pushed."

McCord knew he could, and probably should, have handed the case over to somebody else, but the adrenalin of the chase was already coursing through his veins, dispelling all his tiredness. And he also knew that where there was a body, Amy Thornton would not be far behind.

Chapter 2

As it so happened, Amy Thornton was not on her way home yet but still staring at the cursor on her laptop that had not moved for half an hour.

Her boss and de-facto stepfather John Campbell had finally gone upstairs to the flat he shared with Amy's mother, Valerie. He had kept his office door open all day and come over a few times to ask how she was getting on with her article on Scottish lottery winners, but he was too much of a gentleman to press her about the night spent on the Isle of May. Amy fervently hoped that her mother, who was on a trip to London, had missed the news item about the 'May Ferry Fiasco' as it had been named in the papers that had a penchant for exaggeration. If she found out, Valerie would probably even consider the storm as evidence that McCord was a constant source of danger to her precious daughter and implore her, yet again, to stop chasing criminals. This, in turn, would inevitably lead to another heated argument.

Amy jumped when long, claw-like fingers clasping a large mug of hot chocolate appeared in her line of vision. Without looking up, she took it, careful not to spill any onto her keyboard.

"Thanks, Martin," she said, "but I don't want to talk about it."

She felt her swivel chair being nudged round until she faced her colleague Martin Eden, political editor and John's oldest and best friend. He gave a twirl that sent his kaftan billowing around his long, thin body.

"You haven't said a word about my new outfit, darling," he complained. "I felt I had to express my admiration for the African continent in more than just words."

Amy could not help but smile. Of all the elegant kaftans in the world, Martin had, of course, chosen the most colourful and vibrant garment, which made his naturally pale face look ghostly white. The pointed tips of the sleeves reached down to his knees when he allowed his arms to hang idly at his side, which he rarely did as every phrase he spoke was punctuated by a sweeping gesture.

"Well, as the fashion editor of this esteemed organ, I must say, you are definitely making a statement," she said. "You should ask Mum to take you to one of her fashion shows."

"Oh, really?" he asked excitedly.

Amy shook her head in mock regret.

"No, not really. Mum is a designer of haute couture, as you know full well. Although," she added, "you're certainly gay enough for the scene."

Suddenly serious, Martin wheeled up a chair next to hers and sat down, his jet-black, carefully plucked eyebrows raised up to his hairline.

"You have to tell me about it, darling, or I'm going to spontaneously combust."

Martin had made it his mission in life to advance the romance between Amy and McCord, which he deemed to be written in the stars. So far, he had not had much help from either of them. When he heard of the ferry cancellation, he was beside himself with joy, but had been deeply disturbed by Amy's unhappy countenance when she came into the office that morning. He had been fluttering around her suggestively all day, but she had made it quite clear that she was not going to discuss the matter, especially not while John was about.

Amy took a sip of the sweet, hot chocolate.

"Nothing happened," she said matter-of-factly. "Will you now stop pestering me about it?"

Martin frowned. "I don't understand."

"There is nothing to understand," Amy said sharply. "When are you going you accept the fact that McCord is not interested in me?"

Martin shook his head.

"I am absolutely sure he loves you."

"If he does, maybe he is gay," Amy said.

She sat up. Why had this thought never occurred to her before? It would explain a lot. "I mean, you are gay, and you love me, right?"

"Guilty as charged on both counts," Martin replied. "But McCord isn't gay. I'd know. Tell me exactly how this 'nothing' happened."

Amy shook her head. "Martin, please…"

"I can see that you are upset. Tell me!"

He gripped her hands and stroked her fingers with his thumbs.

Amy sighed.

"We were waiting to be taken back to the mainland when the storm hit. Around ten o'clock, we realised that we would have to spend the night in the bothy there. Imagine: no food, no water, only what we'd taken with us. I thought it was quite romantic, a bit like being shipwrecked, and it was interesting to see how people reacted to the situation. There were no beds, only blankets and six mattresses. I didn't hold out much hope, but most of the others were outdoorsy types, so McCord got me one."

"Ah," Martin interrupted. "See? DI McCord made sure you were comfortable. Possibly even hoping for a wee snuggle on the mattress to keep warm."

Amy shook her head impatiently. "That's where you're wrong. He just lay down on a blanket next to me."

Martin, assessing the situation like a general considering the position of his troops, asked, "How close was he?"

"Not close enough for anything interesting to happen," Amy said.

Martin pointed a bony finger at her. "Did you give him any encouragement, verbal or otherwise?"

Amy snorted. "Of course not. How awkward would that have been for both of us? I'd never put him in a position like that."

Martin tutted. "And don't you think those very thoughts also occurred to him? Do you really think a man like DI McCord is going to make a move in a room with ten other people in it? The first step needs to come from you. The fact that he didn't try anything on is a mark of his respect for you and irrefutable proof that he is madly in love with you!"

Amy pulled Martin's face towards her and kissed him on the forehead.

"You are very sweet. But you are also totally wrong. All he cares about are those blasted birds. I've never seen anybody so excited about an LBJ–" she read the question in Martin's eyes "–a little brown job. Like a sparrow or a wren. No, I've been thinking about my life in general, and my love life in particular, and I've decided that I'm going to try one of those dating apps."

Martin lifted his arms in horror. "Absolutely not!" he shrieked. "You have no idea who you are dealing with online. Any psychopath could turn up to those dates!"

"Don't be such a hypocrite," Amy said. "You date guys from Tinder all the time."

"That is completely different!"

Amy stabbed Martin's chest with a pen.

"And why is that?"

"Because… because… I'm not you, and usually my dates range from disappointing to disastrous. If I had somebody like DI McCord in my life–"

"I don't have anybody in my life," Amy said. "That's the whole point. I'm fed up with drinking G&Ts on my own in the evening."

Before Martin could reply to that, an alert came up on her screen, and she quickly scrolled down the posts.

"What's up?" Martin asked.

"Something's going on at the Crags. Police, ambulance; the full works. It'll be a suicide."

"But it could be a murder!" Martin said hopefully. "You wouldn't want to miss that, would you?"

He didn't need to add what that meant. Seeing Amy hesitate, he picked up her jacket and stretched out his arm. "Off you go, darling. But don't wander about up there on your own, do you hear? Not in this fog!"

Amy took her jacket. Her heart was beating faster, as it always did when a new case was beckoning. McCord had nothing to do with it at all. Or so she told herself.

Chapter 3

Although the scene of the incident was only a few hundred yards away from St Leonard's police station, McCord took his car to the little roundabout behind Holyrood Palace and up the slope towards Salisbury Crags. The rugged, reddish-brown rock face, formed millions of years ago by rising magma forced between layers of sedimentary rock, loomed contemptuously over the tiny humans and their vehicles at its feet. McCord drove as far as he could without ruining the chassis, and killed the engine. The flashing blue, red and white lights were oscillating in the water droplets running down the windscreen. It was like a fairground, without the fun.

McCord stepped out of the car and swore as cold, brackish water seeped into his shoes and muddied the hem of his trousers. Why couldn't people kill each other in heated living rooms?

He greeted the two constables, who had arrived first on the scene and now seemed relieved to be able to hand over to somebody more senior. The younger one, looking barely out of school, filled McCord in on the situation as he was leading him past the waiting ambulance. The fog was rolling down from the top of the cliff and a fine drizzle set about, slowly drenching everybody unwise enough not to wear waterproofs before venturing out. McCord hoped the Crags would not decide to shed any of their rocks onto them while they were walking underneath.

He was guided towards what seemed an oddly shaped boulder, but as he came closer, he saw what it really was: slumped on a mossy rock sat a giant of a man – about a foot taller than McCord and twice his weight in muscle and fat. With his khaki trousers, brown jumper and untamed facial hair, he blended into the surroundings as if he had lived on these hills since prehistoric times.

When McCord carefully approached and the man lifted his head, however, the illusion was destroyed. His face had the unhealthy pallor of a city dweller, and McCord could smell booze and cigarettes on his breath. A sheen of sweat covered his face and neck and his huge, trembling hands dangled uselessly at his sides. He stared uncomprehendingly at McCord.

"Mr Ross Cartwright?" McCord asked quietly. "I'm Detective Inspector McCord. I understand that you made an emergency call earlier saying that you had found a body?"

Without turning, Cartwright pointed to the slope behind him where a dark blue shape was sprawled across the stony ground.

McCord hesitantly raised his gaze to the prone figure. He now regretted arriving at the scene before all the others. A little later, and forensics would have erected a nice white tent that shielded the body from view; he would put on an overall, gloves and plastic overshoes that protected not only the scene from contamination, but somehow also him from the horror he had to face. Dr Cyril Crane, Edinburgh's premier pathologist, would inevitably make fun of him, and his sarcastic remarks would help take the sting out of the disturbing sight. But not today.

He approached carefully, checking the ground for any clues. Two yards away from the corpse, he stopped. Across the short, tough grass battling the elements, long, blonde hair was spread out, covering most of the woman's face apart from the right eye, which was still opened in terror. A trickle of blood had dried on her chin. McCord's eyes quickly moved down the body that seemed strangely intact. She was dressed in expensive-looking jogging gear and wore muddy trainers.

He walked gingerly back down the slope, trying not to slip.

"Can you tell me exactly what happened?"

"It's me wife, Sarah," Cartwright said in a robotic voice. "She fell from up there."

He pointed to the upper edge of the Crags.

McCord decided not to mention Cartwright's earlier suggestion that she had been pushed. It was important not to influence a witness with leading questions.

"You mean, it was an accident?" McCord asked hopefully. Maybe there was still a chance of a quiet evening and an early night.

"I think she was pushed," Cartwright said, his voice thick now. "She screamed."

And then, maybe not.

"I don't understand," McCord said, frowning. "Were you not up there with her?"

Cartwright shook his head. "She was jogging. I couldn't keep up with her."

McCord looked at Cartwright's feet. He was wearing heavy boots. What was he doing chasing after his jogging wife in those?

"I was worried she'd fall," Cartwright answered the question before McCord could voice it. "The path's slippery when it's wet, and the fog's quite thick."

This did not make any sense. How did he intend to stop her from falling by running sixty feet below her?

"You sure you weren't up there with her?" McCord asked again.

"I've already told you I wasn't!" he shouted. "Are you not listening to me?"

McCord ignored his aggressive attitude for now.

"What makes you think she was pushed? Surely, if she slipped and fell, that would also have made her scream out."

"I saw her stop and I had a feeling that there was somebody up there with her."

"You had a feeling?" McCord echoed, wondering now if not only alcohol but also drugs were involved.

"I couldn't see because of the fog, but there was a shape behind her, and then she, sort of, jerked forward and…"

He wiped his face with his hands as if trying to get rid of the vision in his head.

A shape. That was the most insubstantial thing ever to ruin an evening. Next, the guy would claim it was one of the ghosts that were rumoured to frequent the top of the Crags.

"Where the hell are the SOCOs?" McCord asked the constable. After a long Monday following a sleepless night, his patience – never plentiful – was wearing thin.

Right on cue, a couple of vans approached.

"Listen, lad," McCord said to the constable, "get the first responders to have a look at Mr Cartwright, and if he is good to go, take him to the station and get a formal statement from him. And don't forget to give him a cup of tea from the machine."

McCord reckoned that should be punishment enough for Cartwright's earlier rudeness.

He watched them make their way towards the ambulance, the constable offering Cartwright a supportive arm, roughly shrugged off. They passed the leader of the forensics team who, already in his overall, was trudging up the slope towards McCord. The scowl on his face made it clear that he did not relish this occasion either.

The men nodded briefly at each other and introduced themselves.

"Up there," McCord said, pointing to the top of the shelf above them. "The victim's husband thinks he might have seen somebody pushing her down."

"I hate this hill," the leader of the forensics team grumbled. "Good for nothing but scraping bodies off the bottom. Someone should stick explosives under it, blow the whole lot up and put us all out of our misery."

"Now, now," McCord said. "I didn't hear that. Once you are done down here, see if you can find any sign of a struggle up there."

The other man stared at him. "Really? And here I was, thinking I'd clamber up there merely to enjoy the view." With a sweeping gesture of his arms, he took in the thick blanket of greyness that had enveloped the whole city by now. "No, you sit down and relax while we get on with doing all the work."

McCord looked at the damp, moss-covered rock Cartwright had been sitting on and decided to wait in his car. The other constable had secured the whole area with blue-and-white tape, which was just as well, as a throng of curious onlookers had already gathered. McCord's heart skipped a beat as he recognised Amy in the front row, standing on tiptoes and looking around for him. He made a beeline for her and lifted the tape so that she could go through.

"Special permission," he said to the others who had begun voicing discontent. "Please, do not obstruct the work of the emergency services and the police. We'll give an official statement as soon as possible."

He smiled at Amy, but she was not looking at him. Instead, she was rummaging in a large shoulder bag for her notebook.

"What have we got?" she asked, moving out of earshot of the crowd.

McCord shrugged. "Husband called it in. He says he thinks somebody pushed her over the edge, but it's all very vague. Apparently, he was down here and saw a shadow up there with her before she fell or jumped. But why was he not up there with her?" He sighed. "Maybe he is one of those who can't accept the fact that the person they loved died by accident or committed suicide. They feel they should have saved them and can't cope with the feelings of guilt, so they'd rather blame somebody else. Problem is, we have to investigate it anyway."

Amy looked up at the cliff edge.

"It would be a perfect spot for murder, though, especially in this weather. What are their names?"

"Sarah Cartwright; husband's Ross Cartwright. See what you can find out about them."

"That's a first, you asking me for help," Amy said, with a distinct note of satisfaction.

"I'm not asking for help," McCord bristled, taken aback by her cool demeanour. "It's just that Gilchrist doesn't want another body on his books; and he adores you because you always make out that he is the best ever leader of any police department in the country."

Amy looked up, her face red with indignation.

"You know I have to write that; if I didn't, do you really think he would give me access to the station and allow you to share confidential information like that? Besides, he knows that I have helped put a fair number of killers in Edinburgh behind bars since we started working together."

"You seem to labour under the misconception that we can't solve crimes without you," McCord said, angry now himself.

"Well, you can't," Amy fired back. "Or have you found Jai Sandhu's killer yet? If I'd been here when it happened–"

"But you weren't. You were more interested in taking photos of petticoats in Milan."

"Well, then, see how far you get without me this time," Amy said and stomped off.

McCord stared after her, nonplussed. How had this argument come about? He went over the conversation again and again without understanding where it had gone wrong. Maybe he shouldn't have said that about her not solving the cases, but if he had agreed, she would claim next that she had caught all those killers entirely on her own. One had to make a stand, surely. But feeling righteous didn't make him feel any better. Suddenly, he resented this whole investigation. He walked down towards the cars to see if there were any witnesses to the incident, all the while cursing the bent figure of the man who was being coaxed into a police car, cursing Gilchrist and, even more than those two, cursing the whole miserable place that was Edinburgh on a gloomy, wet evening.

Chapter 4

At nine the next morning, McCord called a staff meeting. He had not slept much, but Gilchrist had been on his back already demanding a progress report. The Super loved nothing better than seeing his face on the news, so he had decided to make a public announcement at eleven, appealing for witnesses to Sarah Cartwright's fall.

McCord pinged the metal frame of the incident board with a pen, and immediately everybody went quiet.

"Suspicious death at Salisbury Crags yesterday evening. A woman called Sarah Cartwright fell to her death. The incident was reported by her husband, Ross Cartwright, who claims to have been on the path below the Crags and thinks he saw her being pushed down by a shadowy figure he could not make out. He was under the influence when I spoke to him almost straight afterwards. Forensics examined the spot from which she fell and found no evidence of a struggle. The ground up there is stony, so there are no discernible footprints."

PC Mike Turner's hand shot up.

"We still haven't solved the Sandhu case. We're too short-staffed as it is, so why are we running a murder investigation based on something a drunk thinks he might have seen?"

There was an uncomfortable silence in the room; questioning McCord's judgement was not the done thing in Edinburgh CID. But McCord smiled indulgently. Turner was very young, very keen and had not only shown good judgement before, but also showed the tenacity of a terrier when it came to pursuing a killer.

"Well, I have good news for you, Turner," McCord said. "Superintendent Gilchrist also wants a big push on the Sandhu case. He has organised a TV crew to visit the station to do a re-enactment of the arson attack using the CCTV and information we have. Dharwan, I want you to get the footage ready and sift through the files for material that is appropriate to release to the public. Then contact Sandhu's relatives and warn them that the press is going to descend on them. And while you are there, if they are willing, go over the whole story again with them. We don't want reporters to dig up something that we may have missed."

PC Surina Dharwan nodded, as an excited murmur went around the room.

"But," McCord continued, "don't get your hopes up too much. In all likelihood, this is going to cause us a huge amount of work leading to absolutely nothing."

He pushed away the nagging suspicion that they might have got further with the Sandhu case if Amy had been involved.

"To get back to this new case, there is a distinct possibility that a woman was murdered at the Crags last night, so this becomes our new priority," McCord said. "At the top, forensics found an empty backpack, which belonged to Sarah Cartwright. Her husband says it usually had weights in it, but they were nowhere to be found. The question is, why did she take off the backpack, and where are the weights?"

"Are there any other witnesses?" Calderwood asked.

"The place wasn't as busy as usual because of the bad weather. It was also past six o'clock, so most of the tourists would have left. Maybe Superintendent Gilchrist's appeal later this morning will jog somebody's memory."

McCord looked around for comments. "Yes, Turner?"

"The husband's story doesn't make sense," Turner said. "Why was he there at all if he wasn't jogging with his wife?"

"He says he was worried about her having an accident," McCord said. "Maybe he was going for a walk while she did her round. But I agree with you; his story doesn't sit well with me either."

"But if it was him who pushed her, why would he draw attention to himself?" Turner asked. "He could have just run off and waited for someone else to find the body."

"Could be a double bluff," McCord said. "It wouldn't be the first time. He might have been seen and wants to pre-empt any suspicion. DS Calderwood and I are going to have a look at the victim's flat and have another chat with her husband. Dr Crane promised me the post-mortem report this afternoon; then we'll hopefully know more. But meanwhile, we need witnesses and background on the Cartwrights. Report anything you find back to Calderwood. Special brownie points for progress before eleven o'clock. Off you go."

When McCord opened the door of his office, he was hoping to find Amy waiting for him, but the visitor's seat was empty.

He barely admitted it to himself, but he was disappointed. Usually, Amy's curiosity about a case superseded their quarrels, but not today. Maybe she was still scouring the Cartwrights' social media accounts for juicy titbits.

"So, are we going to the Cartwrights' flat?" Calderwood asked, dragging McCord back to the here and now.

McCord looked out of the window. The fog had finally dispersed, and little patches of blue sky peeked out from behind the fast-moving clouds.

"Might as well," he said unenthusiastically.

* * *

Ross and Sarah Cartwright's flat was only a few minutes away on Prestonfield Avenue. Situated above a

Chinese takeaway on the first floor of an ochre-coloured brick building with a grey slate roof, it was one of the more affordable addresses in this area of Edinburgh.

Calderwood rang the doorbell a few times without success. It was only when McCord began hammering on the door that an angry shout of 'Coming!' announced that somebody was home. Then heavy footsteps and, eventually, the sound of a key turning in the lock. The door was yanked open, and seeing the detectives outside, Ross Cartwright hastily tied his dressing gown, but not before McCord and Calderwood had been treated to a good look at his hairy belly protruding from underneath a Hard Rock Café T-shirt that must have fitted once. McCord was relieved that the man was at least wearing boxer shorts from which nothing was protruding.

"Sorry to trouble you, Mr Cartwright," Calderwood said, with his usual polite smile. He flicked open his warrant card and pointed to McCord. "You met DI McCord yesterday. I am DS Calderwood. I hope we didn't wake you up?"

"No," Cartwright muttered. "I didn't sleep at all last night."

That, McCord believed. There were dark shadows under Cartwright's bloodshot eyes. Whether it was from grief or guilt, McCord was not sure.

"I'm so sorry for your loss," Calderwood continued. "This must be difficult for you, but I was wondering if we could have a look around the flat?"

Cartwright shook his head.

"No point. I told the officers everything last night. You won't find anything here."

McCord was beginning to lose patience with Calderwood's genteel approach to potential murder suspects. A battering ram and threats of arrest were more his style, but he had to admit that Calderwood usually got there in the end, and without incurring a lecture from

Superintendent Gilchrist about the need for Police Scotland to win hearts and minds.

"It might help us to find who killed your wife," Calderwood said. "And that's what you want, sir, isn't it?"

"I've been going over and over that moment ever since it happened, and I don't remember anything clearly. Only her scream and…" Cartwright fell silent and looked as if he was about to cry. "I told him yesterday" – he pointed to McCord – "that I wasn't sure if somebody was up there with her. I could've been wrong. I just want to be left in peace."

McCord, annoyed at the 'him' and fed up with pussyfooting around, stepped forward.

"Well, Mr Cartwright, it was you who suggested foul play in the first place, so we are treating this as a suspicious death. We can either do this now or later with a warrant and another, longer chat at the station."

Reluctantly, Cartwright stepped aside. McCord and Calderwood only just managed to squeeze past him inside the narrow hallway.

The flat was nicely furnished and tidy, apart from an almost empty bottle of Famous Grouse and a tumbler sitting on the coffee table. A large TV screen was mounted on the wall opposite the sofa, and plant pots were lined up on the windowsill, either side of a wedding photograph showing a beautiful blonde next to a beaming Cartwright with much less facial hair.

"What do you do, Mr Cartwright?" Calderwood asked conversationally, although he knew the answer from the entries that the colleagues had made in the file.

"I'm a bouncer at Freddy's, a late-night bar on Frederick Street."

"And your wife?"

"She's… was a manager at Pizza Hut." Cartwright's voice broke.

From a side table next to an armchair, McCord picked up a notepad decorated with Van Gogh's sunflowers.

"That was hers," Cartwright said and made a move to snatch it away, but McCord was having none of it.

He flicked through the pages. Almost all had writing on them; mainly names and numbers – phone numbers, McCord guessed. He looked at the entries towards the end. On one page, the numbers 4 9 15 26 31 + 3 5 had been written down, then each digit had been crossed out and the whole thing underlined three times so strongly that the pen had ripped the page.

"What was that all about?" McCord asked.

Cartwright shrugged. "No idea."

"She was clearly quite excited or angry about those numbers. Strange that she didn't mention them to you."

"Maybe it had to do with work. She didn't talk about her work much."

"And why was that?" McCord asked.

"Dunno. She… ach, what does it matter now?" His voice had turned aggressive again.

McCord flicked back a few more pages and then stopped suddenly.

"She wrote down the word 'police' here. Why would she want to get in touch with us?" he asked.

Cartwright stroked his beard.

"Sarah told me about this one. There had been a break-in at the restaurant, and she had to sort it out. She told me the burglars had been after the cash in the till and when they didn't find any, they took a dozen bottles of booze. Thousands of pounds' worth of damage just for that. Stupid." He shook his head.

"That will all be logged on our system then," McCord said. "We'll need to take the notebook to check out all these names and numbers."

"You can save yourself the time…" Cartwright stopped himself.

"And why is that?" McCord asked sharply.

"Because… because it's all to do with work," Cartwright said.

"We'll see," McCord said darkly. "Where is her other stuff?"

Cartwright led them to the main bedroom and pointed to a large built-in wardrobe. "Right-hand side. And the chest of drawers. She kept her paperwork in the study."

He led the way to the second bedroom. An unfolded sofa bed and a small desk took up most of the space. On the desk, there was a framed selfie of Sarah Cartwright and a plump, blue-haired woman.

"Who is that with her?" McCord asked.

Cartwright's face hardened. "Old school friend of hers."

McCord waited but no further information was forthcoming.

"Does this school friend have a name?"

"Mandy Jackson. Don't know where she lives now. She's a terrible gossip. I wouldn't believe a word she says."

"We'll find her, don't worry," McCord said. "I might find her address in the desk, and if not, we'll get the contact details from your wife's phone."

"Knock yourself out. I'm making a cup of tea," Cartwright said. "Do you want one?" he added as an afterthought.

"No, thanks," Calderwood said. "You should have some breakfast; we'll have a look around here."

When Cartwright had disappeared into the tiny kitchen, McCord said quietly, "Looks like they were not sleeping together. You take the big bedroom. Have a look in the washing basket; our lads last night didn't think to take his clothes and shoes from him for forensics, the idiots. We'll take them today unless he's already put them through the wash, which would be suspicious in itself. I'll see if there is anything interesting in the desk."

Calderwood nodded and left the study.

Sarah Cartwright had been a well-organised woman. Her papers were filed neatly in labelled ring binders, but there were no bank statements. McCord assumed that she did online banking and that all her transactions would be on her laptop, which he bagged.

Half an hour later, they reconvened in the living room where Cartwright was sitting watching the telly, in front of him an egg-stained plate and an empty mug.

Calderwood was carrying a large, bulging plastic bag and a heavy small one.

"What's in there?" McCord asked Calderwood.

"Weights," Calderwood replied.

McCord turned to Cartwright.

"Mr Cartwright, I thought you told us that your wife always took the weights with her when she went jogging?"

"That's right," Cartwright said defensively. "I don't know why she didn't take them yesterday."

"So, you didn't leave the flat together," McCord stated, "because you would have noticed. Did she have a specific route she followed each time?"

"I think so, I'm not sure. She always ran on her own, at the same time."

"Did you not ask her where she went?"

Cartwright's face turned red, but he said nothing. McCord eyed him closely.

"Do you know the password to her laptop?"

Cartwright shook his head.

"We'll take all this with us," McCord informed Cartwright. "We'll give you a receipt, and you'll get everything back in due course."

Cartwright pointed to the large plastic bag. "What are you taking her clothes for?" he demanded.

"These are your clothes and shoes, the ones you wore yesterday," Calderwood said.

"You don't seriously think I killed me wife, do you?" Cartwright shouted. "It was me who called you lot in the first place!"

"It's simply routine," Calderwood said soothingly. "We need to eliminate you from our inquiries. There is nothing to worry about."

But Calderwood's open and honest expression had no effect. Cartwright looked very worried indeed.

Chapter 5

When McCord and Calderwood returned to the station, there was a note telling McCord to go to Superintendent Gilchrist's office asap.

McCord sighed. "What does he want now?"

In Gilchrist's office, he was surprised to find a fresh-faced, buxom woman dressed in a businesslike trouser suit and sensible shoes. Going by the few grey streaks in the short, blonde hair, McCord estimated her to be in her early forties.

"You must be DI McCord," she said, with a warm, firm shake of the hand. "So pleased to meet you. I'm DCI Audrey Hepburn."

She watched McCord closely and seemed to wait for a comment.

Unsure what she expected from him, McCord thought it safest to say as little as possible.

"Ma'am."

A smile that made her unremarkable features suddenly very attractive spread across her face.

"You must be the first not to make a comment about breakfast or a fair lady."

McCord, who had been raised by a resolutely single father without female relatives around, looked at her uncomprehendingly.

"You have a reputation for being difficult to work with, DI McCord, but I can see already that we are going to get on famously. May I call you Russell? My friends call me Heppie, for obvious reasons."

McCord, who detested over-familiarity, ignored the question and instead brought the conversation back to business matters.

"Where is Superintendent Gilchrist?" he asked.

"Oh, haven't you heard? Arthur fell ill straight after the public appeal." She leant forward as if there was somebody else in the room who might overhear. "He was vomiting blood, so he was taken straight to the Infirmary."

"Right," McCord said, wondering if it was Gilchrist's constant irritation with him that had caused a stomach ulcer or if it was the other way round.

"HQ has seconded me here to support you now that you have two unsolved murders on your hands without the superintendent's input and guidance," she said.

McCord wisely suppressed the comment that Gilchrist's absence would only lead to an increase in productivity.

"Right," he said again.

Vomiting blood did sound serious. Maybe, after a long period of recovery, Gilchrist would retire on a comfortable pension…

"It seems, we'll be working together for the foreseeable," Hepburn interrupted his pleasant daydream, "so why don't you get me up to speed over lunch?"

* * *

Back in his Sunset Boulevard an hour later, McCord couldn't wait to pass on the good news to Calderwood.

"Looks like we are rid of Gilchrist for quite some time. He's in hospital with a nasty case of indigestion, so we've got this DCI, Audrey Hepburn, now. She seems alright apart from the fact that she wants me to call her Heppie." He shuddered involuntarily. "No way."

Calderwood laughed. "I can see why, though. Is she a fair lady?"

McCord grinned, but Calderwood knew him well enough by now. He googled the DCI's name and held out his phone.

"Ah," McCord said with a deadpan expression, looking at the movie posters. "Hilarious. Isn't it great that Gilchrist is gone, though?" he added, grinning now. "He's always hated me for some strange reason."

Calderwood smiled. "I think the feeling is entirely mutual, sir, isn't it?"

McCord shrugged. "I suppose so. You were his golden boy, of course, so you'll miss him desperately."

Calderwood ignored the dig.

"By the way," he said, "Cartwright was telling the truth about the break-in at Pizza Hut. The incident was logged on the system."

"That doesn't mean he didn't kill her, though. Maybe the post-mortem will tell us if he did," McCord said.

Calderwood pointed to a note on his desk. "While you were having lunch with the new boss, Dr Crane called. He'll be at the mortuary this afternoon if you want to pop over."

That was not one of McCord's favourite places, but at least now he would not have to watch a skull being sawn open and inner organs being weighed in a metal bowl as if he was at a butcher's shop. He was glad he had eaten his lunch; he knew he wouldn't have much of an appetite after his visit to Cowgate.

* * *

Dr Cyril Crane was in his usual buoyant mood.

"I think you might have got yourself a murder, DI McCord," he said cheerfully. "Come and have a look."

McCord only hesitated a split second, but that was enough for Crane to notice. He guffawed.

"Come on. She doesn't look too bad, even to someone with your delicate constitution. Inside, she is a right mess as you would expect after such a fall, but I've made sure she was sewn up before I called you. She was quite a striking young woman, see?"

McCord did not see.

"What have you found that makes you think it was murder?" McCord asked.

"This." Crane pointed to several smudged bruises on Sarah Cartwright's upper arms. "Somebody grabbed her very tightly."

"Can you tell how big the hands were?"

"Not precisely, I'm afraid," Crane said. "It looks like the position of the hands shifted, so there are no distinct outlines."

"Could she have got the bruises before the murder rather than during it?"

Crane smiled. "This is why you are the detective, not me. If asked in court, I'd say the bruises were sustained at or very shortly before her death."

"Well, well," McCord said. "That's certainly something I'd like to ask her husband about."

* * *

Back in the office, McCord found Amy in an animated chat with Calderwood. She had slipped a white cotton jacket over the flowery dress that he had seen her in before, and he couldn't help noticing that she wore no tights over her smooth, shapely legs.

"I was wondering when you'd turn up," McCord said, attempting a light tone, but the look in her eyes told him that he had hit the wrong note. Again.

"I've got some information pertinent to your inquiry," she said coolly, "and I thought I should share it with you."

Normally, he would have pointed out that this was what the law required rather than a personal favour to him. He also knew that she expected at least the same amount of information in return, but he swallowed the comment that sat on the tip of his tongue.

He cleared his throat, simply glad that she was back on the case. "Yes?"

"I've just spoken to Sarah Cartwright's BFF—"

"What the hell does that mean?"

"Best friend forever," Amy said, rolling her eyes. "You really need to keep up, McCord."

"It's a girl thing," Calderwood explained, coming to McCord's defence. "It basically means a very close, loyal friend."

McCord tapped his fingertips on the desk.

"Thank you for the lecture on the female psyche, Calderwood." He turned back to Amy. "How do you know who her best friend was?" The question was barely out of his mouth when he could have kicked himself for being that stupid. Social bloody media, of course. "Never mind, go on."

Amy regarded him with a mixture of irritation and puzzlement.

"Her name is Amanda Jackson, aka Mandy. I tracked her down in the beauty salon where she works, Tanz, in Craigmillar. Fortunately, they don't only do tanning, but facials as well, so I got Jackson to myself for half an hour. She is one of those who loves having an audience. All I needed to say was 'ooh' and 'aah'."

Calderwood threw McCord a glance, nudging him to acknowledge Amy's awesome efficiency in procuring high-quality gossip, but all McCord said was, "And?"

"She and Sarah knew each other from school. Jackson says that Sarah often complained to her about her husband, who was insanely jealous. I think you should look at the domestic situation there."

McCord sat up. "Did she mention physical abuse?"

"I asked her that, and she said no, not as far as she knew. But Sarah's husband accused her of having a lover and watched her every move. Sarah told Jackson that she wanted to leave him, but she was worried about what he might do."

McCord smiled grimly.

"Excellent. I would like a word with this Amanda Jackson. I agree with you; the domestic angle is the one we should concentrate on."

Amy and Calderwood, momentarily stunned, did not say anything.

"What?" McCord asked.

Amy brightened up. "You are taking my suggestion seriously? That must be another first. Are you feeling quite well?"

McCord was offended. "I've always taken your ideas seriously."

Calderwood emitted a little squeak, began to cough, and covered his mouth with a freshly laundered handkerchief. McCord shot him an angry look.

"It might not always have sounded like that, but I think I am sometimes… misunderstood."

"Right," Amy said.

McCord was not sure whether that expressed agreement or a sarcastic denial, but she was not willing to elaborate.

Instead, she picked up her bag from the floor.

"I'm off. Meeting at the magazine," she said by way of explanation and left the two men; one contemplating the unfathomable mystery that were women, and the other the foolishness of men.

Chapter 6

Half an hour before the end of the day shift, McCord summoned the troops again for an update. He noticed Hepburn standing by the incident board, examining the notes and pictures.

"Please don't mind me, Russell," she said. "Do start."

McCord turned to face his colleagues who had fallen quiet, curiously eyeing the strange woman next to McCord who had the audacity to call him by his first name.

"Okay, everybody, this is DCI Hepburn. While Superintendent Gilchrist is on sick leave, she will be overseeing the investigation."

McCord silenced the murmured greetings and muttered speculation with a wave of the hand.

"What do we know so far about the victim? Turner?"

Turner hastily closed his top button, straightened his tie and stood up.

"Sarah Cartwright, 28, born in Dalkeith; father, joiner, died from cirrhosis of the liver nine years ago. Mother is working at the local baker's."

"Did she say anything about Sarah's marriage or any trouble she might have been in?"

"They haven't been in touch since Sarah finished school and left home immediately afterwards. The mother said she had been against the marriage to Ross Cartwright from the outset, but Sarah had told her, apparently in no uncertain terms, that she was not somebody she would take relationship advice from. According to the mother,

Sarah was always a difficult child and a nightmare as a teenager. As far as she is concerned, Sarah had made her bed, so she could lie in it."

Turner sat down again.

"Charming woman," Hepburn interjected. "Who's been looking into Sarah Cartwright's work life?"

"That would be me, ma'am." Calderwood did not need to straighten his tie; he always looked effortlessly elegant. "I started with her former guidance teacher at Broughton High School. According to her, Sarah was always in trouble until fifth form when she suddenly started to work hard and got five decent Highers, but she didn't go to university straightaway. She worked as a carer and as a waitress. I think she needed to save money because a year later she enrolled in a Business Management course at the Open University. She got her degree two years ago and shortly afterwards became manager of the Pizza Hut restaurant on North Bridge. The staff spoke very highly of her but told me she was disappointed when she was passed over for promotion. That's all, I'm afraid."

"Right," McCord said, taking charge of the meeting again. "We're getting the picture of a hard-working woman who had a very difficult start in life but wanted to make something of herself."

He was aware of Hepburn nodding approvingly, but she did not interrupt. "The post-mortem has revealed bruises on her arms that possibly point to her being pushed off the Crags, but they could also indicate domestic abuse or somebody else being violent towards her shortly before her death. Struthers, you were tasked with gathering witness statements. Where are we on that?"

DS Walter Struthers would not normally have bothered to get out of his seat, but seeing that there was a new boss present, he shot up.

"We've had a couple of calls after the superintendent's appeal, but I haven't managed to follow up on them yet."

"There's a surprise," McCord muttered. "Well," he said in a louder voice, so that everybody could hear, "get onto it. They might have seen something that either corroborates or disproves Cartwright's version of events."

He pointed to the picture of Ross Cartwright that was pinned up on the incident board.

"Everybody else will be working on the husband. I want to know where exactly he spent every minute of the last two days, and I want all their acquaintances and work colleagues interviewed."

"Are we ruling out an accident or suicide then?" Calderwood asked.

"We're not ruling out anything yet," McCord said, "so let's keep an open mind. However, a good friend of the victim has suggested that we should look closely at the husband, and that's what we are going to do. I shall speak to her in the morning and see what else she knows. Any other questions? No? Good. Let's see if we can wrap this up quickly."

When the others had dispersed, Hepburn sidled up to McCord.

"I've been looking at your team and spoken to some of the officers today," she said. "I heard it was your idea to promote Duncan Calderwood to DS after a very short time as a DC."

"Superintendent Gilchrist was keen for him to get on," McCord said, truthfully.

"That doesn't surprise me at all. Arthur has a reputation for mingling with the upper classes."

She wasn't daft, this one, thought McCord.

"I was very happy to support DS Calderwood's promotion because he is one of my best officers."

"Yes," Hepburn said, drawing out the vowel with great scepticism. "But his type often antagonises others."

"And what would be his type?" McCord asked, although he knew what she meant, and a rare flash of self-awareness told him that he had been guilty of the same prejudice when he had met Calderwood for the first time.

"Ach, you know, the posh, public-schoolboy type," she said.

McCord's nostrils flared. "He's not like that."

"But there is a perception that Duncan has had it a little too easy on the way up."

Damn, thought McCord, she must have spoken to Struthers, and he would not have hesitated to grasp this opportunity to blacken Calderwood's name.

"Duncan came in through the accelerated graduate scheme, didn't he?" Hepburn asked.

McCord nodded, suddenly resentful at her dropping Calderwood's hard-earned title. "I don't quite see the relevance, ma'am."

Hepburn gave him a look of reproach mixed with disappointment.

"Heppie, please. Personally, I think it is better, particularly for officers who come from a posh area of Edinburgh and have been privately educated, to spend time on the beat. It grounds them. I am aware that you benefited from the same scheme, but you at least came from a tough background and know what goes down on the mean streets of the city."

She spoke in a soft, melodious voice, but McCord could not allow this veiled attack on his partner to pass. "DS Calderwood worked in Castlemilk. That's as tough as it gets in Greater Glasgow," he said, a little more sharply than intended. "And as you will know, earlier this year, he put his life on the line to protect a member of the public—"

"Without a bulletproof vest and backup," Hepburn butted in, "which shows poor judgement at best. And he indirectly caused your injury, as well. Afterwards, he was on sick leave and reduced hours on full pay for months. Police Scotland doesn't need heroes, Russell. We need well-run departments."

"Hindsight is a wonderful thing," McCord said. "And if DS Calderwood was injured, it was my responsibility. I should have listened to his concerns at the time."

Hepburn regarded him with the same interest as one might observe a newly discovered exotic flower.

"It is unusual for officers in charge to accept responsibility so readily. That does you credit, Russell, but Duncan had gone off on his own accord without consulting either you or Arthur, hadn't he? Which takes us neatly to the next point I wanted to raise with you." She lowered her voice. "What is this I hear about a journalist popping in and out of the station as if she was a member of staff?"

McCord swallowed hard.

"Miss Thornton has hugely contributed to several cases—"

"I understand that she is yet another protégée of Arthur's."

She looked at McCord, inviting confidences about long-held grudges. "You can't have been happy that she gained exclusive access to this station in return for complimentary articles about your boss's leadership."

When McCord said nothing, Hepburn shook her head like a headmistress when her favourite pupil refuses to snitch. "You are very loyal, Russell. But rest assured that Arthur won't hear about anything you tell me. It'll be our little secret."

When McCord did not respond, her face became stern. "I think it's time that things were done with a bit more... rigour here at St Leonard's, and I'm so glad to have your full support."

She gave him an encouraging smile. "It's time you went home. I hear you've been working all hours, day and night. That's not healthy. At least now you have a line manager who cares about your well-being."

"Yes, ma'am."

It had come out without thinking. Cringing inwardly, he left the office with a strange sense of failure and foreboding.

* * *

There were three new messages on Amy's Bumble account; from a fellow journalist, a pastry chef and, giving her a little jolt, a divorced Frenchman who was a tour guide in Edinburgh and wrote sci-fi novels in his free time.

Amy had never met her father, a Parisian who taught her mother French, apart from a few other things, and then left her when she became pregnant. Amy thought she had accepted the fact that she would never meet him and that he was not worth the effort, but on the rare occasions when she allowed her deeper feelings to surface, she saw herself as a tree with only half its roots, inherently unstable; the distrust in men that she had inherited from her mother was like creeping ivy covering the trunk and branches and keeping out the sunlight. In her mother's case, only the gentlemanly and irresistibly devoted John Campbell had been able to restore trust and the ability to love again.

Was her instinctive attraction to the Frenchman merely an attempt to fill the gap her absent father had left or, even worse, was she compelled to repeat her mother's mistakes as so many women do? Suddenly, what had begun as a mere game where she might win a prize seemed fraught with danger.

And yet, almost everybody found a partner online these days, so why shouldn't she? All she needed was a strictly rational approach. What was she looking for? Somebody uncomplicated, cheerful and emotionally intelligent who was as crazy about her as John was about her mother. So, the French novelist was discarded, as was the journalist who, according to his profile, was 'still searching for his true self'. This left the smiling chef, who was pictured among friends raising a glass of wine in a Mediterranean setting and dressed as a giant chicken on a charity run.

Wouldn't it be wonderful to be part of his world? With butterflies in her stomach, she clicked on 'compose message'.

Chapter 7

Amanda Jackson was a provocatively dressed woman with a face skilfully hidden behind several layers of make-up and framed by pale blue hair that was bleached white at the tips and swayed like a curtain in front of small ears decorated with a line of piercings. When she was introduced to Calderwood, her extended eyelashes, which would have made a carpet-brush proud, fluttered excitedly but instantly came to a demure rest under McCord's cool scrutiny.

"Thank you for coming in, Ms Jackson," McCord said, after a glance at the file in front of him.

"Oh, everybody just calls me Mandy."

McCord ignored this. What was it with women demanding to be on first-name terms with him?

"I heard that you were a close friend of Sarah Cartwright…"

Jackson's lips had begun to tremble, so McCord paused to allow her to carefully dab the underside of her lower eyelid. Since weeping females made him extremely uncomfortable, he hoped that the fear of a facial mudslide would prevent her from crying.

Calderwood swiftly moved forward and guided her towards the visitor's chair as if she had gone blind. He was rewarded with a warm smile tinged with sadness.

"…and wondered if you could give us some information regarding her husband, Ross Cartwright?" McCord continued.

"Yes, I certainly can."

From the triumph in her voice, McCord suspected that this interview was the highlight of the week for Jackson, if not the month or even the year. He thought it might be wise to view her opinions with a degree of scepticism.

"What can you tell us about Mr and Mrs Cartwright? Was it a happy marriage?"

"At the beginning, definitely," Jackson said. "Sarah was, like, going through a rough time at home; her dad was a drunk, and he knocked her mum about, like, although he never touched Sarah. You'd think she would have been happy, like, when he finally croaked – I certainly would've – but she took it quite hard. I think she was, like, grieving about the father she never had."

Despite Jackson's abuse of the word 'like' in every sentence, McCord registered her perceptiveness.

"And that's when she met Ross Cartwright?"

There was a slight hesitation.

"Nah, he was around before, like, but they started going out around that time. He'd always, like, worshipped her. She said he made her feel safe. I told her that's not enough. I always knew they weren't right for each other, like, but she couldn't see it."

"You knew her from school, didn't you?"

Jackson nodded.

"Besties, we were, all the way from primary. Thick as thieves. We both, like, messed around in class, but she always got better grades than me. Clever, she was. We were trouble then" – she winked at Calderwood – "and when we turned sixteen, like, I left Broughton High to do my hairdressing course, but she wanted a better life. She had it all, the looks, the brains; it was just her folks that held her back, like. As soon as she was free of them, she was ready to fly."

Calderwood cringed, but Jackson went on unperturbed. "Mind you, all that didn't help her in the end, did it?"

"Why did the marriage not work out?" McCord asked.

"It all went downhill, like, when she started her degree. She was a waitress then, but also still working as a part-time carer for an old lady. I don't know how she did it all, to be honest, and she said Ross kept complaining that she never had no time for him anymore; as if it was her job to entertain him!"

Jackson looked at McCord as if daring him to contradict her, which he had no intention of doing.

"When the manager was off sick for weeks on end," she continued, "Sarah managed the whole restaurant by herself, like, and that's when she realised that she could do much better. Ross was supportive, like, at first, but then, I think, he got worried that she would leave him if she was a successful businesswoman, and that's when all the jealousy started. He kept asking her where she was and what she was doing and who with."

"Did he have reason to be jealous? Was Sarah seeing anybody else?"

"No way. Ross was paranoid. He also went through her things all the time, like. Sarah told me only last week that she couldn't stand it anymore."

"Was her husband ever violent towards her?" McCord asked.

Jackson hesitated. "She never spelled it out, like, but she did say that she was afraid of what he might do if she told him she was going to leave him. I don't think he likes me much and, to be honest, I find him scary, actually, so me and Sarah usually met at my place or in town where we could talk."

"Please think very carefully about my next question before you answer it," McCord said. "Do you think Ross Cartwright is capable of murder?"

Jackson did not hesitate a second.

"I'm sure it was him – he's a right nutter. I really don't understand why you haven't nicked him yet."

"We need to explore all possible avenues," Calderwood intervened.

Jackson's face had softened. McCord decided to leave the rest of the interview to Calderwood. He had a way with women. And with men, come to think of it.

"What was Sarah Cartwright's state of mind in the days before her death? Did you see her then?" Calderwood asked.

"Yes, we had a coffee last week, actually." Jackson dabbed her eyes again. "She was very excited, like. She said she was going to get her own restaurant and her own place. I asked her where she got the money from, and she said she'd won on some… bonds?" She frowned in an effort to remember.

"Premium Bonds?" Calderwood suggested.

She nodded.

"Yeah, that was it."

"So, she didn't seem suicidal to you then?"

"Suicidal? Rubbish. She wasn't the type to top herself anyways, but I'd never seen her so happy. 'Things are going to change,' she said. And then…"

She began to sob.

Quickly, before the floodgates opened, McCord rose from his seat.

"Thank you very much for coming in, Ms Jackson. DS Calderwood will see you out."

* * *

"What do you think?" McCord asked Calderwood when he returned a little while later with coffee and muffins.

"According to her, Ross Cartwright is our man," Calderwood said. "And she certainly knows a lot about Sarah's private life. But she said herself that she didn't speak to him much, so all she ever got was Sarah's side of the story."

There was a polite but insistent knock on the door, and Hepburn entered the Sunset Boulevard.

"Wow," she said, taking in the orange glow. "I'm sure that is good for your mental health. Ah, Duncan Calderwood, the rising star. I've been very keen to have a chat."

McCord searched but could not detect the sarcasm that he suspected had to be in there.

"Very happy to, ma'am," Calderwood said, and for the first time, McCord saw Calderwood's smile bounce off a wall.

Clearly, Hepburn was immune to upper-class charm, which, in itself, was a good thing. But immune to Calderwood? An element of doubt about the new boss began to creep into McCord's mind.

"My, we are very formal here, aren't we," Hepburn said. "I've heard that Arthur was very keen on status. But I'm not. We're all in this together, so please, Duncan, call me Heppie. How are you getting on, Russell?" she asked McCord. "Any progress?"

"Some valuable insight from a friend of Sarah Cartwright's," McCord said. "Apparently, Sarah's marriage was far from perfect, and the husband has always been our main suspect."

"Have forensics come back with anything conclusive yet?"

"Nothing," McCord said. "Apparently, it's relatively easy to push somebody off a cliff without leaving any evidence."

Hepburn turned to Calderwood.

"So, what do you suggest we do now, Duncan?"

Flustered by what felt like a sudden attack, Calderwood stammered, "Eh, we just have to keep looking and hope that he confesses under the pressure of the circumstantial evidence we have?"

"I don't think the taxpayer would be very happy for us to simply pray for success, while a well-paid detective sergeant fetches coffee and cake because the fare at the canteen is not palatable enough for some. Walter mentioned that this happens quite frequently. I hope you at least didn't delegate the job to a female PC."

"No, ma'am," Calderwood said, blushing. "Of course not."

"There's no 'of course' about it, Duncan. If you had served in the rank and file, you'd know that these attitudes are still commonplace among men. And now that you are refreshed, maybe you can get up and look for evidence that helps us put a wife-killer behind bars. Good day, gentlemen."

When the door closed firmly behind her, Calderwood turned to McCord.

"Am I being oversensitive, or does she have a problem with me?"

"She's got a chip on her shoulder where upper-class men are concerned," McCord said. "But it's all Struthers' fault. He's been stirring ever since Hepburn arrived. I'm sure, in time, she'll come to appreciate you."

"Let's hope she's quicker off the mark than you were, sir," Calderwood joked.

"What on earth do you mean?" McCord asked. "I realised after five minutes you were a decent copper even if you are a posh git."

"Thanks," Calderwood said. "I think."

"Anyway," McCord continued, "I've been meaning to ask you something. Do women really tell their female friends everything? And I mean everything?"

Calderwood smiled. "I'm sure some of them do."

McCord shuddered. "Do you think Dharwan tells her best friend everything about you?"

Calderwood shrugged. "Surina is not somebody who confides easily in others. But I'll do my damnedest to make sure she has nothing to complain about where I'm concerned."

"So, things are going well between the two of you?" McCord asked.

"Yes. I've actually been wondering if I should pop the question."

"Good," McCord said. "It wouldn't do to have a dalliance between a senior officer and a PC right under my nose. You need to think of her reputation as well. She has a very promising career ahead of her."

Calderwood's face turned maroon. "I am thinking about that, sir. I would never—"

McCord raised his hands in appeasement. "I know you are a decent guy, Calderwood. All I'm saying is, I don't want a love drama hampering my investigation."

Satisfied that he had done his duty as the superior officer and entirely oblivious to the irony of his remark, he opened his emails and whooped.

"Ah, Sutton has something for me!"

* * *

DC Heather Sutton, commonly referred to as 'Heather the Hacker' by her colleagues, did her magic surrounded by several layers of defensive structures which only McCord was ever invited or willing to enter. Even Superintendent Gilchrist was afraid of her. Rather cowardly, or wisely, he had left it to McCord to conduct her last annual review meeting, which was completed in less than thirty seconds and consisted of five words: 'Everything okay, DC Sutton?' – 'Yes.'

McCord had then ticked boxes, invented more elaborate comments and sent the whole lot to Gilchrist, who signed it off with a sigh of relief. This was the only time in the year when Gilchrist seemed happy about McCord's presence at Edinburgh CID.

McCord suspected, however, that DCI Hepburn would not approve of such shortcuts. Maybe he should warn Sutton of a very long, supportive meeting.

He made his way into the inner sanctum with due care and found his most ingenious and socially incompetent officer, self-cut hair pointing in all directions, hunched over her keyboard. She was typing at a speed that would have made a world-class pianist hang their head in shame.

"Unexplained payments into Sarah Cartwright's account, last two months," Sutton said in a husky voice that was never given a chance to warm up.

Her printer spat out a bank statement. McCord grabbed it and read, a frown forming on his forehead. "Two deposits per month. Two different banks. From Daniel Slater, reference 'business'". He looked at Sutton. "Nine thousand nine hundred pounds each time? That's quite a sum – and a strange amount."

"Banks only check deposits over ten thousand pounds. Money laundering or tax avoidance," Sutton explained in her inimitably concise way.

"Could this have come from Premium Bonds? Or any other source?"

"No."

And with that, McCord was dismissed, without being able to broach the difficult subject of DCI Hepburn and her appraisals.

Clutching the printed sheet, he hurried back to his office.

"Calderwood, we've got something–"

McCord broke off when he saw who was sitting in the visitor's chair. His heart seemed to expand in his chest and restrict his breathing.

"Amy has come to see if we are any further with charging Ross Cartwright," Calderwood helpfully intervened.

"I wanted to make sure you weren't fobbing me off yesterday," Amy said. "Police Scotland are not known for high conviction rates in domestic abuse cases. And we all know where that led to last time. I do hope you're taking this one more seriously, seeing that you've got a new boss who is female."

"And who, more to the point, is not enamoured with the idea of a journalist roaming around the station. We need to be much more discreet in future, at least while Hepburn is here," McCord said, having regained his ability to speak and already beginning to get annoyed. "For the record, I am taking the domestic situation very seriously. In fact, we've got a promising lead. Apparently, Sarah Cartwright didn't tell her BFF" – he mimed quotation marks in the air – "everything after all."

"Really?" Calderwood asked. "What has Sutton dug up?"

"She's found the source of the money for Sarah Cartwright's new business venture. Not Premium Bonds, but a guy called Daniel Slater."

"Daniel Slater? That name sounds familiar," Calderwood said. "But I can't place it."

McCord shook his head. "I've never heard of him."

Amy looked at them in turn.

"Are you being serious? Daniel Slater was all over the news a few months ago. He won 7.8 million pounds in the lottery. I interviewed his girlfriend only last week for my article on Scottish lottery winners."

"Why not the man himself?" McCord asked.

"Yvonne Dunbar, that's the girlfriend, says he's quite shy and embarrassed by all the media attention," Amy said. "Lucky for me, she isn't. She's loving it. I'm seeing her again the day after tomorrow to confirm the draft. Did you know that, when asked ten years after they hit the jackpot, the vast majority of lottery winners say that the money changed their life for the worse? Early days for Slater yet, but the fact that he doesn't want to be a celebrity is a good sign. I do hope to meet him next time. According to Dunbar, he is the nicest guy you can imagine. Caring, down to earth–"

"Quite a catch then," Calderwood commented with a side glance at McCord.

"Oh, I wouldn't dare cross Yvonne Dunbar," Amy said with a mischievous smile. "Actually, his is quite a touching story. Absent father, alcoholic mother. She died when he was fourteen. Went to foster parents until he was sixteen, and after that started work as a carer. Then, boom, he's a multimillionaire at the age of twenty-five."

"So, what's he paying Sarah Cartwright twenty thousand pounds a month for?" McCord asked.

"Maybe he was investing in her new venture? Maybe he recognised a similar story and wanted to give her a leg up?"

"Getting his leg over, more like," McCord said. "Maybe Ross Cartwright was right about Sarah having an affair. Let's bring both Cartwright and Slater in tomorrow."

Chapter 8

The following morning, McCord met with Hepburn to appraise her of any progress made. To his dismay, this was to be a daily or, in case of rapid developments, twice-daily affair. Eventually, after repeated admonishments to make sure his team worked as hard as he did, McCord was released.

At the top of his to-do list was to speak to Dharwan and go through the edited Sandhu file that she had prepared for the STV programme, so he summoned her to his office.

"What did the family say about the re-enactment when you saw them?" McCord asked. "I feel sorry for them, having to go over that whole business again."

"Actually, they are relieved that we are still working on the case," Dharwan said. "They knew that the investigation had stalled. The sisters are prepared to give an interview to urge anybody who knows anything about this to come forward. They need closure."

"I don't believe in the concept of closure," McCord said. "This idea that everything is alright as long as you find out how and why is an illusion. Even if your brain understands, the pain never goes away."

He felt Dharwan's eyes on him, affectionate and sympathetic. She knew that his mother had died giving birth to him and that to this day he was trying to atone for his presumed guilt by hunting down killers.

"I suppose the pain is always there," Dharwan said, "but at least you can start to learn to live with it somehow."

McCord cleared his throat. "Did the sisters come up with anything new at all?"

"One of them did. It's bound to be a coincidence, but it is very strange."

Apart from closure, another thing McCord did not believe in was coincidence.

"Yes?"

"Sarah Cartwright was a regular customer in Sandhu's shop."

He leant forward.

"What?"

Dharwan nodded.

"When her picture was on the telly during Superintendent Gilchrist's appeal, one of Sandhu's sisters recognised her. She'd met her once in her brother's shop and he had told her that she came into the shop at least once a week. The sister remembered because Sarah Cartwright was a beautiful woman, and she thought that her brother had taken a shine to her. She said she wore a wedding ring, though, so for him that was the end of it."

McCord jumped out of his seat and began to pace the floor, thinking aloud. "Maybe that wasn't the end of it! Cartwright and Sandhu might have had an affair. We know that Sarah's marriage wasn't wonderful, and Sandhu would not have admitted to the affair to his sister, would he?"

"I wondered about that, but it was about two years ago," Dharwan said. "The sister wasn't sure exactly. But there was no mention of Sarah Cartwright after that, and the sister had never seen her again until the appeal. I can't see a link to his murder or hers."

"The affair might have gone on in secret for years. Maybe Ross Cartwright eventually found out and killed first Sandhu and then his wife?"

Dharwan shook her head. "I don't think so. Sandhu lived above his shop in a busy area. He was serving customers from seven in the morning until seven at night. Most of his free time was taken up with his football friends. Somebody would have noticed, but when we interviewed them all, nobody mentioned a girlfriend. Sarah Cartwright didn't even live in the same area."

"What was she doing in his shop then?" McCord asked.

"She was a part-time home care assistant at that time. I checked. The old lady she was looking after lived nearby, so she was probably doing some shopping for her. There is another problem with your theory, though."

"Which is?"

"Ross Cartwright is well over six feet tall. Our techies say that the person who was caught on CCTV doing the graffiti and pouring petrol through the letter box is between five foot ten and five foot eleven. It wasn't Ross Cartwright."

McCord had stopped pacing. He slumped back into his chair and sighed.

"Pity. For a moment I thought we had solved both cases at once."

Into the brooding silence that followed, the office phone rang. It was Jack Carruthers, the duty sergeant, to let him know that the STV reporters had arrived. McCord heaved himself out of the chair with a groan.

"Well, let's hope that this is not the complete waste of time I expect it to be."

To McCord's relief, the person in charge of the filming was a pleasant and efficient guy who spoke and moved fast. He clearly had no intention of hanging around longer than necessary. The second guy was stocky and dressed in jeans and a black hoodie. Despite the balmy temperature, he was carrying a puffer jacket and a large sports bag, which led McCord to the conclusion that he would be playing the arsonist's role in the re-enactment later that night. He immediately tried to chat up Dharwan but was firmly put in his place.

The interviews were conducted by a breezy young woman who laughed too much but had come prepared with a sheet full of sensible questions. She was delighted by Dharwan's news that the sisters of the victim were prepared to give them an interview that afternoon.

Hepburn, hovering on the periphery of the proceedings, was very complimentary about the way things were going until Calderwood phoned ten minutes before his interview slot to say that he would not make it back in time.

She took McCord aside.

"Where is he?" she asked McCord angrily. "I thought it would be obvious that this takes priority."

"I sent him to get a formal statement from a couple who came forward after our witness appeal about the Cartwright murder," McCord said quietly, "and on the way back he's had to deal with a lost child who was wailing for his mother, apparently."

Fearing this would be another black mark against Calderwood's name, he added, "Initially, I had assigned the job to Struthers, but he didn't do it. He's such a—"

McCord broke off as the reporter approached. Hepburn simply shook her head and moved out of the way.

When the microphone was stuck in his face, McCord was nervous at first, but he soon got caught up in the details of the Sandhu case and spoke passionately about their efforts to find the killer. Dharwan then went on to describe the devastating impact the murder had had on the family and the local community who were still in deep shock.

Hepburn finished off with a few words. McCord noticed that she didn't have Gilchrist's gusto when dealing with the press or the public and that she was barely able to hide her nerves. But she had dressed up for the occasion and got through it without a hitch. Before McCord had even looked at the clock, the crew were packing up.

When he heard his office phone ring, McCord sprinted back. Carruthers announced the arrival of Daniel Slater, who had readily agreed to come in to speak to McCord.

"Excellent. Thanks, Jack."

He stepped out of his office, curious to meet the millionaire who had had such a tough start in life. Just like McCord and Calderwood always did, Daniel Slater had taken the stairs rather than the lift and was ambling along the corridor with a strange gait that reminded McCord of a rolling ship staying the course despite being buffeted by a storm.

Before McCord had reached him, the TV crew rushed out of the open-plan office, and the female reporter accosted the young man, who didn't look best pleased.

"You are Daniel Slater, aren't you? The lottery winner? Why are you here at St Leonard's police station?"

Slater began to stammer and ran a hand through his strawberry-blond hair.

"Hang on," McCord shouted at them from a distance. "You have no business bothering witnesses who have come of their own accord to help us with our inquiries. You were invited to prepare for the re-enactment of the Sandhu case, which is done, so please leave now!"

Roused by the racket, a few officers, among them Dharwan, had gathered in the corridor, and now Hepburn herself appeared, her face flushed with embarrassment.

"I must apologise for the rudeness of my staff," she said to the team leader. "But DI McCord is quite correct in pointing out that Mr Slater has come in voluntarily to do his citizen's duty. This is not the time nor the place to ask a witness for an interview. We very much appreciate your cooperation on the Sandhu case, but now I must ask you to leave."

The team leader motioned to the reporter to switch off her microphone and lifted his hands apologetically. "I'm sorry, ma'am, if we overstepped the mark. We'll be off then."

Hepburn smiled. "I'm looking forward to watching your programme. PC Dharwan, please show our guests out."

What she meant, of course, was to watch them and make sure they didn't roam or question anybody who had not been briefed.

As Dharwan led the group away, Hepburn turned to Daniel Slater.

"I am so sorry about that, Mr Slater. The timing was most unfortunate."

Slater nodded gravely.

McCord motioned his witness towards the door of his office. For a moment, he feared Hepburn would follow them to supervise their conversation, but she only gave him a brief nod and walked back down the corridor.

McCord closed the door and examined Slater. About the same height as McCord but broader, he stood in the middle of the room, patiently waiting to be invited to sit. Amy was right; there was no sense of arrogance about his sudden turn of fortunes, but rather a desire to please.

"Have a seat. Do you know why I've asked you to come in today, Mr Slater?" McCord asked.

Slater lowered himself onto the visitor's chair, looking worried.

"I should've come to you straightaway, I know, but my girlfriend… And I also didn't want Sarah's husband to pay me a visit, if you know what I mean."

"I have no idea what you mean," McCord said. "Can you explain why you transferred almost forty thousand pounds into Sarah Cartwright's bank accounts?"

Slater looked up, eyes wide. "Because we were lovers, of course."

"Tell me how that came about," McCord said. "You are already in a relationship, and she was married."

"Marriages can be broken, and relationships can be very unhappy, DI McCord," Slater replied with a sad smile. "Sarah's husband is a brute; the only reason she was still with him was that she was afraid of him. And Yvonne, my girlfriend–" he hesitated as if reluctant to say anything negative about her "–she changed after I came into all that money."

"What do you mean, 'changed'?" McCord asked.

Slater sighed.

"All she can think about is what she could spend my money on."

"But you were quite happy to spend twenty grand a month on a lover?" McCord said, unimpressed.

Slater's face took on a wistful expression.

"Sarah was different. She wanted to do something with her life, not just sit by a pool sipping cocktails. At first, she didn't want to take my money. But I persuaded her in the end. I wanted her to be free and independent so she could start a new life, hopefully with me, but definitely without her husband."

Slater paused and looked beseechingly at McCord.

"Was it my fault?" he asked quietly. "Did Cartwright find out and kill her?"

"We don't know yet," McCord said. "Where were you when Sarah was killed?"

"On Monday night, I was setting up the games room in our new house," Slater said. "From the moment we moved in, Yvonne's been badgering me about a billiard table. She thinks it's a must for posh people. Like us." He gave an ironic smile. "She doesn't get it. I'm not posh. I'm just rich because I got lucky. It was a right pig to set up – the table, I mean; it took me ages because Yvonne was no help at all."

"Do you have any idea why Sarah would go jogging in that horrible weather?" McCord asked.

"She was a bit of a fitness fanatic," Slater said. "She didn't care about the weather. She told me once that she had to get out of the house as much as possible, to get away from her husband."

"Do you have any idea why she would carry an empty rucksack?"

Slater shrugged. "I have no idea. Maybe she was planning on getting some shopping on the way back."

McCord was annoyed that this had not occurred to him before.

"I'm afraid, Mr Slater, there is not much chance of getting your money back," he said. "It'll be part of her estate, which her husband will inherit."

"Really? Even if he is convicted of her murder?" Slater asked.

"That's a big if," McCord said. "You'd have to ask a lawyer. But thanks for coming in; you have cleared up a few things for us. I'll take you across to PC Turner, who will take a formal statement."

Out in the corridor, they bumped into Carruthers, the duty sergeant, who was leading Ross Cartwright towards them. Swearing under his breath, McCord gave Carruthers the death stare. He was supposed to always announce visitors before bringing them up.

Ross Cartwright stopped in his tracks and fixed Daniel Slater with bloodshot eyes. "That's him, isn't it?" he yelled.

McCord quickly stepped between the two men and lifted his hand in an imperial gesture. Cartwright was towering over him, still staring at Slater, who looked terrified.

"Calm down, Mr Cartwright," McCord said in a low voice. "I won't have a fracas here outside my office."

On hearing the commotion, Turner appeared from the open-plan office.

"PC Turner, please take a statement from Mr Slater," McCord said.

Turner took in the situation in a flash. He swiftly led Slater towards his desk.

"You coward! Get back here!" Cartwright shouted. "I've seen you on the telly. You're the one who won the lottery! And now you're here because you were having it off with me wife!"

The door to Hepburn's office flew open. Without a moment's hesitation, she stood next to McCord, squaring up to the giant who was shaking his fist in Slater's direction.

"Mr Cartwright, you will accompany DI McCord quietly to the interview room, or I'll have you arrested and put in a cell. Is that understood?"

Cartwright, his eyes still on Slater until he was out of view, reluctantly descended the stairs ahead of McCord. On their way down, they met Calderwood, who was running upstairs, taking two steps at a time.

"Ah, Calderwood," McCord said. "Glad to see that you can join us. Are you sure you've finished babysitting?"

"Sir," Calderwood protested, struggling for breath, "I could hardly–"

McCord's phone rang. "What now?" he muttered, looking at the screen.

It was Amy.

He signalled to Calderwood to take Cartwright downstairs and pressed the green icon.

"Hi," Amy said, without waiting for him to answer. "I've found out something very interesting."

"That's great," McCord said, "but I'm kind of busy at the moment–"

"It won't take a second. Remember Mandy Jackson, Sarah Cartwright's BFF? She used to be Ross Cartwright's girlfriend."

There was a pause.

"And?" McCord asked, decidedly underwhelmed by this revelation. "I take it that was before he married Sarah Cartwright?"

"Yes, but don't you see? Jackson was always in Sarah's shadow. Sarah was smarter, more beautiful, and then she goes and takes Jackson's boyfriend off her as well."

"That was years ago. And why would she accuse Ross of murdering Sarah if she still carried a torch for him?"

Amy sighed. "Ever heard of 'Hell hath no fury like a woman scorned'?"

McCord felt a headache coming on. Amy's Byzantine take on human interactions always left him befuddled. What was wrong with straightforward relationships?

"You are not seriously suggesting that Jackson killed Sarah Cartwright?"

"Why not? She has lied to both of us, hasn't she?"

"She didn't mention it," McCord corrected her.

"Same thing," Amy said. "Does she have an alibi?"

"I have no idea. Listen, I've just had confirmation that Sarah Cartwright had a lover, your nice millionaire, as it happens, and that her husband knew about it. A few minutes ago, he almost assaulted Slater. I'm about to interview Cartwright, again, and I want a confession from him before he has time to think. Bye."

"But–"

"Must go."

He hung up and took a deep breath. It was time to pile on the pressure.

Chapter 9

As they entered Interview Room 1, McCord told Cartwright to sit down, while Calderwood prepared the recording.

"I only had one question for you, Mr Cartwright," McCord said after the preliminaries, "but you have already answered that comprehensively upstairs. You knew that Daniel Slater was your wife's lover."

Cartwright opened his mouth to protest but was silenced by a wave of McCord's hand.

"See, Mr Cartwright, this is what it looks like to me. Your wife was fed up with your jealous and controlling behaviour and began an affair with another man. Did she tell you that she was going to leave you?"

"She didn't!" Cartwright shouted. "I didn't even know—"

"You'd better come clean now," McCord said. "Judges tend to be lenient with people who confess and show remorse."

Cartwright banged his fist on the table, which wobbled alarmingly.

"I have nothing to confess! You can't arrest me for loving me wife!"

"No, but we can for murdering her," McCord said.

"I didn't!" Cartwright shouted.

"Your relationship with Sarah had broken down. We know this because in your flat it was obvious that you were sleeping in different rooms. We know from a reliable witness that you are a very jealous and potentially violent man."

Cartwright's face flushed as he struggled to restrain himself. "But–"

"Then who do we find at the scene of Sarah's death with no reason for being there at all?" McCord continued mercilessly. "You, of all people. Giving us a load of bull about an unrecognisable shape in the fog. How stupid do you think we are? Do you seriously think you're going to get away with this?"

"You have no proof!"

"We will get it," McCord answered. "In the meantime, do not leave town without notifying us."

"I'm going to get a lawyer!"

"Feel free, Mr Cartwright. You'll find there's a row of defence lawyers' offices right across the road from this station."

Calderwood terminated the interview, and McCord led Cartwright towards the exit. He was sure the TV crew would still be hanging around outside, and he wanted to see Cartwright's reaction to their questions.

But at the front door, he found they had encircled Daniel Slater, like a pack of hounds their prey. McCord shot a glance at Cartwright; he made no move to attack Slater this time and was standing back, merely watching the encounter with narrowed eyes.

"Why have you come to St Leonard's, Mr Slater?" the female reporter asked.

"I'm helping the police with their inquiries," he said, echoing McCord's words from before. "And I'd rather not comment."

"Are these inquiries into the Cartwright case?" she persisted.

"Yes."

Slater was beginning to look uncomfortable.

"How are you connected to the case?"

Slater blushed.

"Eh…" He turned as if looking for help and spotted McCord and Cartwright behind him. "No comment," he said. "Excuse me."

The TV crew moved aside, and he walked briskly through the door towards the car park.

The reporter now registered Cartwright and clearly couldn't believe her luck.

"Mr Cartwright," she said, approaching him. "Are you a suspect in your wife's murder case?"

"I shouldn't be," Cartwright announced with a hostile side glance at McCord. "I never killed me wife. Why don't you ask the guy who just left?"

The reporter got so excited, she almost hyperventilated.

"Are you suggesting Daniel Slater killed your wife? Why would he do that?"

Anger and humiliation flashed across Cartwright's reddening face. "No comment."

With that, he pushed past them and rushed off towards the car park.

Calderwood had joined McCord. "Should we not go after him?"

McCord shook his head. "I'd love to, but we have nothing on him that would satisfy the procurator fiscal. Anything from the witnesses you spoke to?"

"It was a couple who were walking their dog up the far end of the Crags when they heard a scream just after five thirty. The wife remembered the exact time because she had just checked her watch. They wondered about calling 999 but then they decided it might have been a bird screeching, and they didn't want to cause an unnecessary call-out. Because of the fog, they didn't walk any further but turned back towards Hunter's Bog, so they were not aware of the emergency services arriving at the Crags. They only remembered the incident when they saw the appeal on TV."

"Wait," McCord said. "When did Cartwright report the incident?"

"A few minutes before six, I think."

McCord did a quick calculation. "Twenty-five minutes. Enough time for Cartwright to run down the Crags, check that Sarah was dead and prepare for the grieving widower performance. It all fits."

"Shame the couple didn't see anybody up there," Calderwood said.

"Forensics haven't come up with anything from the crime scene either and there was nothing at all on Cartwright's clothes. I've checked the phone records again; Sarah Cartwright never contacted Slater by phone. She must have been terrified of Cartwright finding out. The best we can hope for at the moment is that Cartwright confesses. If he's asking for a lawyer, that's unlikely, though." McCord sighed. "But you haven't heard Amy's latest. She's got Mandy whatshername in the crosshairs because she used to be Ross Cartwright's girlfriend." He laughed at the absurdity of it.

"It's odd Jackson didn't mention that before," Calderwood said. "Nor that Sarah had a lover. And what she told us about Sarah's money was also wrong. So, either Jackson's been lying, or Sarah did not confide in her as much as she suggested. Whichever it is, she's turning out to be a very unreliable witness. Maybe what she told us about Ross Cartwright isn't true either. We only have her word for it that he was insanely jealous."

"Not true. Daniel Slater said the same," McCord said. "And you should have seen Cartwright kicking off earlier. He's got some temper on him."

"Still, I think we should bring Mandy Jackson in again," Calderwood said. "If this ever gets to court, we can't have all sorts of surprises coming out when she's on the witness stand."

"Waste of time," McCord said. "Without hard evidence, there won't be a trial at all."

They were walking back towards the office in silence.

"What's on your mind now?" McCord asked.

"I know that you have Cartwright as the killer," Calderwood said, "but let's assume for a moment that Cartwright didn't kill his wife. Who else had a strong motive to get rid of her?"

McCord stopped in his tracks. "Slater's girlfriend! They're not married, and depending on how long they were together, the law may not regard her as his common-law wife either. If Slater had left her for Sarah, she'd have got none of his money, and from what Slater is saying, money is very important to her. On the other hand, Slater says she didn't know anything about the affair."

"I dare say, many men think that and they're usually wrong. Women know when there's something going on," Calderwood said.

McCord nodded.

"Right. Let's bring her in as well. My money is still on Cartwright, but we have nothing on him, and we need to exclude all other possibilities. And then, we'll have to wait for him to make a mistake."

Chapter 10

"Good morning, my precious," Martin greeted Amy when she breezed into the office of *Forth Write* magazine the following day. He was foaming the milk for a latte from a top-of-the-range coffee machine, but his eyes were fixed on Amy. "Once I'm finished here, I want to hear all about your date!"

"How the hell did you find out about that?" Amy asked, dropping her shoulder bag on the floor next to her desk and starting up her computer. "Are you following me around?"

"Only looking out for you," Martin said. "I tried to call you last night, and your phone was switched off. You never switch off your phone, so something very unusual and interesting that was not news-related must have happened. How did it go?"

"Great, actually. A very nice guy. Easy to talk to, good fun, handsome, and he makes the most amazing Danish pastries."

She laughed as Martin's face fell. "Sorry. I know you were hoping for a creepy fifty-year-old who had faked his ID."

"So, when am I going to meet this Prince Charming?" he asked.

"Not until our relationship is strong enough to survive a meeting with you," Amy retorted. "And don't you dare tell John or my mum about this."

"My lips are sealed," Martin said. "Valerie would be thrilled to learn he's not a detective but would resort to thumbscrews to make me reveal every tiny detail about him. And my resistance would be very weak."

"That's exactly why I don't want her to know. Poor Douglas would have two people stalking him."

Martin's face lit up.

"Ah, Douglas. What's his surname?"

"Nice try," Amy said. "Do you not have any work to do? John might be easy-going, but he'll still want something he can print in the next edition."

"He would want me to make sure you are alright," Martin said, putting down the latte on her desk. "The next edition comes a very poor second to that."

"I'm fine. Let me remind you that I am not thirteen years old. And now, I'm busy writing my article. Go away."

Martin sighed and turned away to make another coffee.

"Ah, the cruel rejection of love."

* * *

At five minutes to eleven, Amy was driving her mother's vintage MG down Morningside Road looking for the house number of Gordon McPhail, a past lottery winner who resided in this leafy district of the city, when a billboard outside a newsagent's caught her eye.

'Millionaire in coma after car crash' screamed the headline. She stepped on the brakes and, accompanied by a furious honking of horns, mounted the pavement. Ignoring the stares of outraged residents, she stopped right in front of the shop and darted inside. The picture on the front of the *Edinburgh Evening News* showed Daniel Slater's silver Porsche upside down in a field. The caption underneath read 'Lottery winner's fortunes turned'. Amy grabbed a copy, threw a pound coin on the counter and rushed back to the car. She was desperate to read the article, but she had to move her car before some officious traffic warden could give her a ticket. And, of course, she was already late for her interview, which John had exhorted her never to be.

Tapping her fingers on the steering wheel, she waited for a gap in the traffic, turned back onto the road, and a few yards further down, drove through the iron-wrought gates of a Georgian villa.

McPhail had been on the lookout for her and was not best pleased that she was late. He complained that people always assumed he had nothing better to do than stand around and wait for them. After all, he was doing her a favour, not the other way round.

Amy knew for a fact that he had indeed nothing better to do since he had given up his job as a plumber the day after claiming his win. She also suspected that he was gagging for an opportunity to talk to somebody who was professionally bound to show an interest in his story. And it turned out that she was right.

After being presented with a Glasgow Rangers mug filled with a builder's brew, and a plate of digestive biscuits, she took a seat in a living room that looked as if it had been decorated and furnished by the previous owners and since been left to fade.

McPhail slumped into the armchair opposite her and took a noisy slurp of his tea. Amy had barely taken out her notebook when he began to pour out his heart.

"'Your life will never be the same,' the lottery people said. And boy, were they right. My so-called friends all turned out to be leeches; the wife went off with some foreign bloke along with half my money, and the neighbours are looking down their noses at me."

It took McPhail over half an hour to air all the wrongs that greedy and disloyal people had committed against him. Eventually, he seemed exhausted by his rant. "So, you see, it's been a curse," he concluded, "and I wish I'd spent the money for that lottery ticket on a pint down in my old pub."

Amy was not about to cry. She had a fair idea of the value of the property they were sitting in and could contrast it with the damp community hall she had recently visited, where residents, not rich themselves, had set up a food bank for those people who were struggling to feed their families. And yet, she felt a degree of sympathy for the man. He had moved less than a mile from his original home but, being lost and lonely, as he sounded, he might just as well have landed on a different planet.

"Why don't you get involved in some charity work?" Amy asked. "You would meet very nice people, and it would..." Give your life some meaning, she wanted to say, but that seemed too unkind. "...make you feel better."

He gave a derisory laugh. "I'm not giving my money to scroungers who've never done a decent day's work in their lives! I've always worked hard for my money..."

After another tirade, during which Amy's thoughts repeatedly returned to the folded-up newspaper in her bag, she extricated herself from the charms of her host and sought refuge in her car. She had hoped to be able to read the story there and then, but he stood at the door, waiting for her to leave, so rather than risking another verbal onslaught, she drove off intending to find a parking spot in one of the quiet residential streets, but there was none. She eventually had to stop in front of somebody's drive, hoping they remained unaware or would be in a forgiving mood.

She pulled out the newspaper and unfolded it.

> *Police have confirmed that the driver of the silver Porsche Panamera that skidded off Old Dalkeith Road shortly before 1pm yesterday and ended up on its roof in a neighbouring field, was Daniel Slater, 25, who won the National Lottery earlier this year. His partner, Yvonne Dunbar, 24, spoke to us from the Royal Infirmary intensive care unit. Understandably, she is in deep distress. 'He's had surgery and is still unconscious,' she told us. 'But the staff here are wonderful. All I can do is pray that he wakes up soon.'*
>
> *Mr Slater, who grew up in the Granton area of Edinburgh and worked as a home carer before he hit the jackpot, almost missed out on his 7.8-million-pound win because he had mislaid the ticket that changed his life. We asked the officer in charge whether excessive speed was a factor in the crash but were told that the investigation into the causes of the accident is still ongoing.*

Amy lowered the paper. The irony of finding the mislaid ticket, only to be almost killed by the very thing he bought with the proceeds, did not escape her. She had been due to meet Yvonne Dunbar, his girlfriend, that very afternoon, but now she would be in the Royal Infirmary at the bedside of her boyfriend who was fighting for his life. The well-brought-up part of her urged Amy to give the distressed girlfriend some privacy, but her long nose twitched with the scent of a story much bigger than the psychological effects of suddenly coming into a lot of money. She flung the paper onto the passenger seat and headed east towards Little France.

Chapter 11

Walking along the familiar corridors with their competing smells of disease and disinfectant, Amy contemplated the fact that this was the third case that had led her to the ICU and the bedside of an unconscious man. This time, however, there were no complicated feelings involved other than curiosity and compassion. Daniel Slater, unusually lucky after an inauspicious start, deserved to pull through and be able to enjoy the trappings of a carefree life.

Amy hoped that either Fiona or Cathy were on duty. During her frequent past visits, she had established a good rapport with both nurses and rated her chances of getting a little extra information about the patient out of them.

She rang the bell.

To her disappointment, an unfamiliar male nurse opened and asked who she wanted to see.

"Hi, I'm Amy Thornton. I wonder if I could speak to Daniel Slater."

"Are you family?" the nurse asked.

"Not exactly, but I was meant to meet him this afternoon."

Well, it was at least potentially true.

"I'm sorry, only family members are admitted. His partner is with him at the moment."

The nurse was clearly anxious to get back to his patients, but Amy was not willing to let him go just yet.

"How is Dan?"

"I'm afraid I can't give out personal information," he said. "You'll have to wait until he has been moved out of the assessment unit and into a ward."

The door closed.

Amy knew when she was beaten, but as she was about to leave, she noticed a young man who was slowly approaching the door of the ICU. He stood for a moment with his finger almost touching the bell button only to let it fall by his side again.

Amy moved a step towards him.

"Are you alright?"

The man turned. He was about a head taller than Amy and bulging muscles strained against the sleeves of his polo shirt. Amy guessed he was in his early twenties. Without any attempt at delicacy, he examined Amy from head to toe, taking in the olive-skinned face that would have been stunning, had it not been for the slightly too long, aquiline nose, and the petite figure, accentuated by a tailored linen suit whose pale yellow contrasted beautifully with the dark, shoulder-length hair. He made no attempt to hide his appreciation either, breaking into a toothy smile.

"I'm fine, thank you. Richard McAllister."

He held out his right hand and shook hers firmly.

"Amy Thornton. Nice to meet you. Are you visiting somebody?"

"My brother Dan," he said with a glance at the locked door. "Do you know him?"

Amy stared at Richard McAllister. "Daniel Slater is your… brother?"

He lifted his hand in an apologetic gesture.

"Half-brother, to be precise. I know, we look nothing like each other."

Strange, Amy thought, that Yvonne Dunbar had not mentioned a brother.

"How do you know Dan?" McAllister asked.

Amy never liked to tell people that she was a journalist; on hearing that, they either clammed up or insisted on telling her their life story, depending on whether they wanted to see their face in print or not. But there was no way round it now.

"I'm with *Forth Write* magazine. I was supposed to show his girlfriend a draft of our interview later this afternoon but then I read in the paper that Dan had an accident, so I came straight here. They won't let me in because I'm not family, but I'm so worried about him. Would you mind if I waited here until you come out again?"

"We'll see," Richard McAllister said cryptically and pressed the bell.

It took a while for the door to open, and the same male nurse as before stood in the frame, looking harassed.

"Can I help you?"

"Yes, I'm Daniel Slater's brother and I was wondering if I could see him."

The nurse threw a surreptitious glance at Amy, clearly surprised to see her still there. She wondered if he suspected a ploy on her part to gain entry by deception.

"What's your name?" he asked McAllister.

"Richard, eh, Ricky. Ricky McAllister."

"Give me a moment. I'll see if Mr Slater is awake."

The door closed again.

Richard McAllister gave Amy a little smile and raised his eyebrows. She assumed he was nervous about the state he might find his brother in. Judging by the picture of the Porsche in the paper, one would not expect Dan to be sitting up in his bed, ready for a game of canasta.

They waited in silence. The next few minutes seemed a very long time, and McAllister was bouncing up and down on his heels when the door opened again. The nurse looked uncomfortable, and Amy's stomach contracted.

"I'm afraid you can't see your brother, Mr McAllister."

Amy slowly rose from her seat, expecting to hear the worst, but McAllister shrugged as if he had expected this answer.

"How is he?"

"He is out of danger for now. But he's very drowsy."

McAllister scrutinised the nurse's solemn face. "He doesn't want to see me." It was a statement rather than a question.

"I'm sorry," the nurse mumbled and shut the door.

McAllister remained standing where he was, momentarily lost in thought.

Seizing the opportunity to find out more, Amy coaxed him towards the seats. He followed as if in a trance and sat down next to her.

"Why does your brother not want see you?" Amy asked. "You don't seem that horrible a person to me."

McAllister could not help giving a little laugh.

"There's a difference between being a horrible person and having done something horrible, my therapist kept telling me. She said we all do bad things at some point in our lives but it's what we do about it that matters."

"She was right," Amy said, wondering what a confident, perfectly healthy-looking young man needed a therapist for.

"I've tried to make amends!" McAllister jumped up, suddenly agitated. "I wrote to him on his eighteenth, thinking this is a milestone when you can leave all this childhood crap behind – sorry."

Amy waved his apology away. "No, it doesn't quite work like that," she said, thinking of her father.

"And then again on his twenty-first," McAllister continued, "and then again when I read about the lottery win. I thought now that he finally got lucky and had a great life, he would… but no. Not even after he almost died."

Amy was about to ask what terrible deed he had committed against his half-brother when he suddenly got up. "This is no use. I need to do something, not just talk and write pathetic letters. I'll go to the police."

"What for?" Amy asked, intrigued. "Don't you believe it was an accident?"

McAllister sat down again.

"I haven't been in contact with Dan for years, but this is not like him. Speeding recklessly along a country road? Dan is the most careful person I have ever known. He was always writing lists of what needed to be done. Always tried to get it right and blaming me for getting things wrong. Used to drive me crazy." He laughed and seemed lost in memories for a few seconds. "No, I can't see it."

"Suddenly coming into money does strange things to people," Amy said. "Believe me, I've spoken to a few of them. He bought a Porsche, after all, not a Ford Escort. Maybe he underestimated the power of the car and got carried away."

"Dan never got carried away, never, not even when things were awful…" He broke off, as if suddenly aware that he had said too much. "Sorry about bending your ear. I was—"

"No need to apologise," Amy said. "If you like, I'll talk to the police. I have contacts there. And if I get the opportunity to speak to your brother, I'll ask him exactly what happened. Do you want to give me your number, and I'll let you know what comes up?"

"That'd be great," McAllister said, his face lighting up.

Amy typed his number into her contacts. He seemed nice and was far more attractive than Douglas and the other guys on the Bumble profiles she had been looking at. Normally, she would have sent a text to pass on her number, too, but the mention of the therapist and his cryptic remarks had made her think. Maybe it was wise to check him out first.

"There we go," she said brightly, slipping her phone back into her bag before he could ask for her number. "So, back to work now?"

He nodded.

"I mustn't be late. First proper job after graduating. Somehow everybody seems to think I need taking down a peg just because I've been to uni but don't know anything about the job yet."

Amy smiled. "I think that happens a lot. What do you do?"

"Chemical engineering," he said.

"Well, you'll certainly know more about that than most people. Good luck."

"Do call me, please."

He gave her a little wave and hurried towards the exit.

Amy sat back down and pulled out her phone. McCord answered after the second ring.

"Hi. Everything okay?"

McCord always seemed to assume that she must be in trouble. He was almost as bad as her mother.

"I've got news," she said. "Daniel Slater has been in a car accident. His Porsche came off Old Dalkeith Road and landed upside down in a field."

"I know. It was flagged up on the system. Is he alright?"

"He's in the ICU in the Royal Infirmary."

"Which, I assume is where you are, too. You really have a thing for men on life support, don't you?"

Since McCord himself had been one of them, she was momentarily at a loss for words.

"Is that it?" McCord asked.

Amy, thinking he was referring to the 'thing' she might have had about him, was flustered. "What do you mean?"

"Your news. Slater is not exactly our main worry."

"Maybe he should be," Amy said.

McCord sighed.

"Don't start," she snapped.

"What?" he asked, all innocence.

"That patronising thing you do. 'Oh, it's one of Amy's outlandish theories again.'"

"That's not true," McCord said although it was exactly that. "Let's hear it then, what did you find out?"

"Slater has a half-brother Yvonne Dunbar told me nothing about."

"Is she obliged to tell you everything about his private life?"

"No, but it's weird she didn't mention him at all. The brother turned up today, but Slater refused to see him. Apparently, Richard McAllister, that's the brother, did something terrible when they were children, but he wouldn't tell me what."

"How dare he. Well, I suppose, that'll keep you busy for a while."

Amy tried to hide her rising irritation. Not only with him, but with herself for needing him to take her seriously.

"That's not all."

"Good grief, there is more?"

"McAllister said it's completely out of character for Slater to speed in a way that would cause such an accident."

There was a brief pause in which McCord seemed to process the remark.

"You don't buy a Porsche to cruise along at forty miles an hour," he said eventually. "Maybe the half-brother doesn't know Slater very well, or he has changed. Money does that to people."

"That's what I told him," Amy said, "but I think we should look into that accident."

"We?" McCord echoed. "I think you mean I should use the overstretched resources of the homicide unit to investigate a car crash?"

"Oh, well, please yourself."

Furiously, she stabbed the red icon.

* * *

At St Leonard's, McCord looked at Calderwood.

"She hung up on me!"

Calderwood shook his head. "Of course she did. The same old story. She gives you intel, and you poo-poo it."

"Yes, but this time it does border on the ridiculous. A twenty-five-year-old lottery winner crashes his new Porsche on Old Dalkeith Road. Not much mystery in that, is there?"

There was a polite knock on the door and Dharwan stuck her head into the office.

"DCI Hepburn wants to see you, sir."

She flashed a quick smile at Calderwood and disappeared again.

McCord sighed and made his way across the corridor where Hepburn was pacing up and down.

"Russell, thanks for coming over so quickly. Have you seen the STV news?"

Surely the re-enactment had not been broadcast yet, McCord thought. "No, I've been pretty busy."

"There was an item about Daniel Slater's car crash. How he was interviewed in the Cartwright case here at this station; how he was subsequently threatened by Sarah Cartwright's husband and accused of being her lover. How both men left the station at the same time, and fifteen minutes later, Slater's car comes off the road, and he ends up in intensive care. What a disaster!"

"Yes, it was unfortunate–"

"Unfortunate?" Hepburn's voice had become shrill. "Do you know what we'll get when the tabloids jump onto the bandwagon tomorrow? 'Police introduce husband of murder victim to her lover'! 'Millionaire chased off the road by lover's husband after police interview?' And so on and so forth! They'll have a field day with this!"

Hepburn stopped to look pleadingly at McCord.

"Russell, please tell me that this was a simple car accident and had nothing to do with Ross Cartwright!"

"There is no evidence to suggest that it was not an accident," McCord said.

"That won't do," Hepburn said. "I want evidence either that it was an accident, or that it was somebody else who drove Slater off the road. I want this story to go away. Make that your top priority!"

"Ma–" – he saw the hurt look on her face and took the plunge – "Heppie, both the Sandhu and the Cartwright murders are still unsolved–"

"This is my first high-profile case, Russell. I need this out of the way before the re-enactment is broadcast, or they'll drag this up again on prime-time TV, nationwide!"

Hepburn looked as if she was about to cry, and before he could be caught up in that, he muttered a promise to do his best and withdrew.

Chapter 12

McCord returned to his office in a white-hot rage.

"Hepburn wants me to investigate this stupid car crash! Never mind the two unsolved murders. No, she's worried about what might be in the papers and what it'll do to her precious reputation!"

"She has a point, though," Calderwood said. "If Cartwright put Slater in hospital after finding out here at the station that he was his wife's lover, we're in trouble."

"I don't care about the papers," McCord said. "We are homicide detectives, not bloody PR agents."

"Of course, we are," Calderwood said soothingly. "But I think, even if her priorities are wrong, Hepburn is right that we should look more closely into this accident."

"Really?"

"Don't you think it is an odd coincidence that a lottery winner who has been linked to a murder victim is now in ICU?" Calderwood asked.

It occurred to McCord that this was the second coincidence in this case. First, Sarah Cartwright had been a regular in Sandhu's shop, and both had been murdered. And now her lover was in intensive care.

"Okay," McCord said, exhaling noisily. "I give in. Phone Traffic and find out what happened on Old Dalkeith Road."

* * *

Fifteen minutes later, Calderwood put the receiver of the office phone down.

"They're still analysing the tyre tracks, but it looks like Slater suddenly swerved off the road."

McCord frowned. "Could have been the brakes."

"Yes, but there's the timing as well," Calderwood said. "He crashed shortly before one o'clock."

"When did he and Cartwright leave the station?"

Calderwood flicked through the case notes. "Our interview with Cartwright was terminated at 12.35. It would have been quarter to before they both left. Cartwright could have followed him in the car and driven him off the road." He looked up. "And we let them both go after Cartwright threatened him. If he almost killed Slater, we bear some of the responsibility."

"We had no reason to hold Cartwright," McCord said, who had had the same uncomfortable thought. "But they should never have met at the station, I agree. Let's hope Traffic can sort this out quickly."

"Not likely," Calderwood said. "Apparently, there are no traffic cameras or CCTV near the site of the accident, so we can't prove anybody else was there."

"I love the way you always cheer me up," McCord said.

Calderwood ignored him. He was reading a message on his phone.

"I'll just shut up until you've sorted out your online social life, shall I?" McCord asked.

"Sorry, sir, I've just got a message from Amy. She's following Yvonne Dunbar on X, and a woman called Kimberley MacLean has posted a nasty message asking why Dunbar stands by her man if he has fathered a child and never paid any child maintenance, and that she is just, quote, a whore staying with him because of his money."

"I'm told X is full of crackpots and liars," said McCord, who had so far steered well clear of the site.

Calderwood shrugged.

"Possible, of course, but there's a picture of a cute baby boy with the post. Amy says she'll get onto it."

McCord drummed with his fingers on the desk.

"Why did she tell you and not me?"

Calderwood merely shook his head.

* * *

At three o'clock, McCord called a team briefing. When he went through to the large open-plan office, he walked past Hepburn who was standing at the door and gave him a conspiratorial smile. He had hoped that she might have missed the memo about the briefing. He found that the colleagues spoke much more freely without her there, but Hepburn was far too hands-on to allow that. Besides, she had a lot riding on this.

The mood was subdued, and everybody fell quiet without him needing to raise his voice.

"Right," he said. "I assume you have all heard about Daniel Slater's car accident yesterday. We are going to make this our top priority."

"What?" Turner burst out. "What about Sandhu and Sarah Cartwright?"

McCord looked sternly at him, suppressing a smile. After all, Turner had merely said out loud what everybody else was thinking.

Turner cleared his throat. "Sorry, sir."

"As I was saying," McCord continued, "we need to find out whether it was nothing more than an accident or if somebody forced Slater off the road. The papers have got hold of the story that Cartwright met Slater here at the station just before the crash, and if he went on to almost kill Slater" – he threw a glance at Hepburn – "we will get the blame. So, it would be handy if we could either prove it was an accident or that somebody else did it. Traffic says the only tyre tracks on the road are from Slater's Porsche."

"It must have been an accident, then?" Turner asked hopefully.

"It is still possible that somebody overtook Slater and came so close to him that he pulled the car over and lost control. That could have been done with or without malicious intent."

"But who apart from Cartwright would want to frighten or kill Slater?" Turner asked. "We checked his background. According to his former colleagues, he would give Mother Teresa a run for her money. All his home-care patients adored him, especially the old ladies. Couldn't do enough, apparently. Two of them even left him something in their wills."

"Hm. Isn't that a bit suspicious?" McCord asked.

"There was never any hint of foul play if that's what you mean. They were relatively small sums, certainly not worth killing for. A couple of hundred pounds in one case, and five hundred in the other, over the course of eight years. Also, one of his former colleagues said that he was annoyed rather than pleased and said people would think he did the job for the money, and it made him look like a scammer."

"Was there any suggestion that the relatives of his patients were unhappy with him?"

"Nothing that I could find," Turner said. "It seems that most of his clients were lonely, and they loved having him around." He looked down at his notes. "One relative, who was too busy to look after his elderly mother, called Slater a 'godsend'."

"Well, he wasn't exactly a saint, though, was he," McCord said. "He cheated on his girlfriend with Sarah Cartwright and deposited large sums of money into her accounts. And there is the possibility that he fathered a child and never paid up. If somebody tried to kill him, I think the motive lies in his private life."

He pointed to the picture of a grim-looking Ross Cartwright on the incident board. "What have we found out about him so far?"

"He was following Sarah around a lot," Dharwan said. "Her colleagues noticed him turning up unannounced at her workplace, especially if Sarah was staying on late. Once he got into a fist fight with a customer who was talking to her outside the restaurant. The customer can't have pressed charges, though, because there is nothing on the system. On the day of the murder, Cartwright was caught on CCTV following her towards the Crags. Sarah was about eight minutes ahead of him by that time. She was jogging, and he couldn't keep up."

McCord frowned.

"So, how could he possibly have caught up with her?"

"Sarah would have run a loop, so if he knew or guessed her route, he could have waited for her on the way back."

McCord nodded.

"Anything else?"

"The CCTV is too blurry to be sure, but it looks as if she is carrying an empty backpack."

"Yes, we know she left her weights at home. Maybe she was going to get some shopping on the way back. Good work, both of you," he said to Turner and Dharwan.

"We're saying that Cartwright killed his wife and then went after her lover," Calderwood said. "But would he have been stupid enough to attack Slater straight after their run-in at the station with a dozen police officers and a TV crew as witnesses?”

“People do stupid things when they are angry,” Turner said with an air of authority gained by experience.

“We need to find out if he has an alibi,” McCord said. “Calderwood and I are going to pay him a wee visit tonight.”

Calderwood’s face fell.

“I know,” McCord said. “Kiss goodbye to your weekend off.”

If Dharwan was disappointed, she didn’t let it show.

“What about Slater’s girlfriend?” she asked. “She can’t have been happy about Slater cheating on her.”

“Agreed,” McCord said. “We need to speak to her as well. Dharwan, see if you can get her in today, if possible.”

“Since we’re talking about women with a motive, how about this Kimberley MacLean?” Calderwood asked. “If Slater is the father of her son, he would inherit millions on his death because he has no other close relatives.”

“Do we have any more information on MacLean or her son yet?” McCord pointedly asked Calderwood.

“Not so far,” Calderwood replied.

“Anyway,” McCord continued, “Slater does have a relative. What about his half-brother, this bloke Richard McAllister, who turned up from nowhere the minute Slater was about to croak it? Would he have a claim on the estate?”

“Probably not over the child,” Calderwood said. “I’ll find out.”

“McAllister wouldn’t have known about the boy. He told Miss–” McCord noticed Hepburn straightening up and caught himself in time “–we’ve got it from a reliable source that he and Slater hadn’t been in touch for years. Turner, I want some background on him.”

Turner nodded.

McCord rubbed his temples, where a nasty headache was beginning to form.

"Let's hope that they were all in a meeting of the Women's Guild or having tea with a vicar during the accident." Conscious of Hepburn's presence, he left the next sentence unsaid. He dismissed his team, knowing that they were thinking the same – once this blasted accident was out of the way, they could finally get back to their two unsolved murders.

"Well done, Russell," Hepburn said when everybody had gone back to their workstations. "Mike Turner and Surina Dharwan seem very keen and capable."

"They are."

"I didn't see Heather Sutton at the meeting. She is supposed to be here, isn't she? I was hoping to have a word with her."

"She is here," McCord said, "but she tends to stay at her workstation. She doesn't like talking to people."

"That's a peculiar attitude for a police officer, isn't it?" Hepburn said with a frown. "The way things are done at this station is very strange. I was under the impression that Arthur ran a tight ship, but it seems I was wrong."

Thinking of Gilchrist, McCord became aware of an unfamiliar sensation: a sense of nostalgia.

"DC Sutton is—" he scoured his memory of the latest training session "—neurodiverse," he said proudly. "She works best on her own, but she has excellent IT skills."

That was putting it mildly, but McCord didn't like to think what Hepburn would say if she found out just how good Sutton really was.

"I understand," Hepburn said. "Thank you for alerting me to this. I'll bear that in mind when I do her appraisal. It's important to me that all members of my team get the support they need."

* * *

McCord was in his Sunset Boulevard pondering how he could protect Sutton from Hepburn's 'supportiveness' when Struthers knocked on the door.

"Yes, Struthers?"

Struthers pumped up his chest and stood in front of the desk looking down on him. "Yet again, you haven't given me a task in line with my rank. Superior officers are not supposed to have favourites, are they, but you do. Just because Calderwood is posh and Dharwan is a dish, they shouldn't get all the glory. It's not fair."

McCord told himself to stay calm. The Equality Act mentioned race, religion, sex, age and, more recently, gender reassignment, but not stupidity. To McCord, this type of discrimination constituted good management of human resources.

He pulled a piece of paper from his desk drawer and wrote numbered instructions on it.

"I've got a very important task for you right here, Struthers. First you find the make, model and registration number of the cars belonging to Ross Cartwright, Yvonne Dunbar, Richard McAllister and Kimberley MacLean. Then find out where they were at the time of the Slater's accident."

Struthers looked doubtful, and McCord was sure that he had forgotten who Kimberley MacLean was.

"The woman who claims that Slater fathered her child," McCord explained, summoning up his last shreds of patience. "I want those registration numbers tonight."

As Struthers was leaving the office, Calderwood appeared with a cardboard tray containing two coffee cups and two muffins. Struthers shot him a venomous glance. "It's alright for some," he hissed, but McCord had heard.

"Just get on with your job, Struthers," he snapped.

Calderwood closed the door behind Struthers and put the goodies on the desk.

"I hope Hepburn didn't see you?" McCord asked. "I'm beginning to feel like a criminal in my own station."

He took the first bite of his lemon muffin and pulled out the witness statement from the farmer who had been first on the scene at the car accident. He said he had been ploughing the other end of the field when he heard the crash. Looking round, he saw the Porsche turning on its roof and shuddering to a standstill on the fresh furrows. He could not remember any other vehicles on the road, but he had been facing the other way and would not have noticed a second car passing at the time of the crash.

The report from the traffic police was lengthy but inconclusive. McCord flung it down so vehemently that it almost slid off the desk. What was he now, a traffic warden? And at the same time, Sarah Cartwright and Jai Sandhu lay in the morgue, waiting for justice. Something had to be done.

Chapter 13

Amy was standing half-naked on plastic sheeting, with Amanda Jackson pointing the gun at her. She fervently hoped her sacrifice would be worth it. And that John would accept this as part of her expenses.

"Are you sure now that you don't want your face done as well?" Amanda Jackson asked. "It's the same price."

"No thanks," Amy said.

Being sprayed into the face with some brown gunge was one step too far, even when investigating a murder.

"Shame. You have such beautiful skin. I've always wanted to treat a client with olive skin, and here you are!"

Jackson's enthusiasm did not reassure Amy in the slightest.

"Here we go! Keep nice and still."

A cool mist descended on Amy's back in slow and regular movements. Jackson seemed to know what she was doing, after all. Amy relaxed a little and waited until the beautician had moved round to her front. She wanted to observe Jackson's reaction to her next comment.

"Have you heard?" Amy asked with a breathless voice that came from trying not to move, but sounded suitably excited. "There's a rumour going round that Sarah Cartwright had a lover who paid her oodles of money every month!"

The spray gun jerked in front of her shin, but the curtain of blue hair obscured the view of Jackson's face.

"That's a lie!" she burst out. "Sarah would have told me! We were best mates!"

Jackson was putting on a good show, one had to give her that.

"I'm not surprised you're upset," Amy said with a sigh. "But that's just typical of these women who have it all. Brains, beauty, an adoring husband, and then chucking him away for a millionaire… nothing and no one is ever enough for them."

Jackson had begun to cry. "No!"

Almost there. Just one more nudge.

"Personally, I've got some sympathy for people who hated her… oh my God, what are you doing?!"

Looking down, Amy had caught a glimpse of her legs. They were orange. "Put that stupid gun down, now!" Amy shouted.

Suddenly Frank Sinatra's velvety voice invited them to come fly with him, while Jackson shrieked, blindly fumbling with the switch of the gun. Eventually, she managed to stop the spray but not until Amy's feet and the floor were covered with tanning fluid. Jackson dropped the gun and scrambled to get to her phone on a shelf behind the plastic sheeting, but before she could reach it, the voice recorder had kicked in.

"Listen, I want this sorted tonight. It's mine, and you know it. That was the deal. No more putting it off. Your place, in an hour."

The following bleep reverberated in the sudden silence.

"What was that all about?" Amy asked.

"Nothing, just my boyfriend," Jackson said hastily.

"That didn't sound like a boyfriend – hey, what are you doing now?"

Jackson was frantically rubbing oil that smelled strongly of coconut onto Amy's legs.

"They're going to sack me," she sobbed. "Only yesterday, I broke a customer's nail, and the boss gave me hell! If you keep putting oil on your legs and soak them in a hot bath at home, it'll take the worst of it off. I hope," she added bleakly. "Please don't tell my boss!"

Amy fought down a mild panic. The oil didn't seem to make any difference whatsoever to her glowing legs. But she also sensed an opportunity here.

"What's the story with this boyfriend?" she asked. "Is he threatening you?"

Jackson sniffed. "No, no, it's fine, really. I won't charge you for the treatment, of course, just please don't tell my boss! And I need to tidy up this mess before I leave!"

"Alright," Amy said soothingly.

She might look like a hairless orang-utan, but through the sickening wafts of coconut she'd caught a different scent. Boyfriend, aye right. She would make McCord eat his words when she presented him with the killer of Sarah Cartwright. In less than an hour.

* * *

McCord had not long returned from a walkabout in the station to see how the information gathering was progressing when the office phone rang.

"A Ms Yvonne Dunbar is here to see you."

"Thank you, Jack. Show her up."

McCord was impressed. He had not expected her to come in so promptly, but Dharwan had delivered again. He went out into the corridor to watch her approach. The way somebody walked into the station often told him a lot about a person.

The officers in the corridor stopped and stared as the young woman made her way towards McCord. She minced along on her stiletto heels in a pink dress that was a little too tight and low-cut to be classy. Golden curls bounced angrily off her shoulders, and a glittering handbag was swinging impatiently from her wrist.

"Good afternoon, Ms Dunbar. This way, please."

"I really don't know why you've asked me to come here," she said, revealing the kind of snow-white teeth that would set ordinary people back a couple of months' worth of rent. "If this is about the accident, your colleagues have been in touch already. Dan had comprehensive insurance. I should be at the hospital. If they call me, I must leave immediately, just so you know."

McCord inhaled noisily. He was not in the mood for entitled snootiness.

But before he could vent his feelings, Calderwood stepped in. "Please have a seat, Ms Dunbar. We appreciate that you have come in at this difficult time. We need to ask you a few questions about that accident," he said.

"What questions? Dan came off the road, probably avoiding one of the potholes that the council can't be bothered to fix."

"There are no potholes on that stretch of the road," McCord said. "According to the investigator's report, the skid marks indicate that Mr Slater lost control of the vehicle and then veered off the road. Is he a fast driver?"

She shook her head. "He isn't reckless, if that's what you are implying. Is this about the insurance?"

"It's about a potential murder attempt, Ms Dunbar," McCord said.

"Murder? Don't be absurd. Why would anybody try to kill Dan? He is the sweetest guy you could meet!"

Calderwood examined his shoelaces, but McCord held his eyes fixed on Dunbar.

"You can't think of anybody who might hold a grudge against your boyfriend?"

"Of course not. He is such a caring person. You know, he is still visiting old clients of his, from the time he was a home carer. There was this old lady… when she died, he was the only one who went to her funeral. She even left him a little something in her will because he had been so good to her. And so she should, because she was a right besom, always complaining. That's actually how we met, Dan and me; I was working at the dentist she went to. What was her name… Margaret something–"

McCord held up his hands, stemming the tide of random memories. "Ms Dunbar, we are investigating the possibility that somebody forced your boyfriend off the road. Is there really nobody you can think of who might have done that?"

Dunbar looked at him with wide-open eyes, as if suddenly inspired.

"Maybe that crazy woman who claims that my Dan is the father of her little brat? When I think about it, she actually threatened us, but I never thought she meant–"

"How did she threaten you?"

"Three days ago, she turned up at our home with a toddler in tow, just like that, and demanded to see Dan. I told her he was out and asked what this was about. She said the boy is her son and Dan's the father, and that she never got a penny in maintenance. But now she wants him to pay up, and all the arrears as well." She was growing agitated as she spoke. "She's such a liar. Me and Dan have no secrets, so I told her to get lost. Then the wee toerag started howling, and I could just see our nosey neighbours pricking up their ears in the garden next door, so I took my phone out to call the police. She didn't like that idea because she stormed off saying if Dan didn't get in touch, we'd be sorry."

"Have you had any contact with her since?"

"No. Well, she left a vile comment on X, but there are always people who can't bear others to be happy, aren't there? When I told Dan, he said she was making it all up and to ignore her. But now she's even gone to the police with those ridiculous allegations."

"She didn't come to us, actually," McCord said. "We heard about it from a different source."

"Who?" Dunbar asked.

"If Mr Slater did a paternity test," Calderwood interjected, distracting her from her question, "and it was negative, this whole problem would go away, surely."

"Dan is still not well. He is barely conscious and needs complete rest to get better, the doctor says. But I expect you to punish that woman for what she did."

"We don't know yet if she has done anything," McCord said, "and, anyway, it is not our job to punish people." Seeing Dunbar was about to protest, he added quickly, "We'll have a word and check her alibi for the time of the accident."

Then, watching her closely, he asked, "Do the names Sarah and Ross Cartwright mean anything to you?"

Dunbar frowned. "No, I don't think so. Wait... Sarah Cartwright... was she not the woman who fell off the Crags? It said in the *Daily Mail* that the husband might have pushed her, poor thing."

"So, you didn't know that Sarah Cartwright was Mr Slater's lover and that he transferred forty thousand pounds into her bank accounts?"

Dunbar froze, and it took her a few seconds to recover. "Don't be ridiculous. There must be some mistake. Me and Dan love each other, we're very happy; there's no way—"

"He told us about the affair himself," McCord said.

"You are lying!" She began to cry.

McCord continued, ignoring Calderwood's reproachful looks. "Where were you on Monday evening between five and seven? And yesterday around one o'clock?"

"Where was...? You can't seriously believe that I–"

"I don't believe anything, Ms Dunbar," McCord said. "I'm gathering facts and evidence. So, I'm asking you again, where were you on Monday when Sarah Cartwright was murdered, and yesterday when Mr Slater had an almost fatal accident?"

Dunbar wiped away her tears, leaving some of her pale skin exposed, while the edges of her face remained a dark beige. Then she pulled herself up and gave McCord a look of pure hatred.

"On Monday evening, I was... I was out shopping," she said.

"Alone?"

"Yes," she hissed. "And yesterday, I was at home when I got the call."

"We need the names of those shops," McCord said.

"I'll write out the list downstairs," she said. "I'm not staying here a minute longer than I have to, you horrible little man!"

And with that, she teetered out of the office.

When the door had slammed shut behind her, Calderwood sighed.

"Let me guess," McCord said. "You think I was too hard on her."

"Her boyfriend is in a bad way in hospital, and you pull her in, tell her of his affair and then accuse her of murdering the lover and trying to kill him? She seemed genuinely distressed."

"It was your idea in the first place," McCord said, unrepentant. "And I'm beginning to believe there could be something in it. What she says doesn't add up. Why does she pretend her relationship with Slater was wonderful when we know it wasn't? And" – he rifled through the growing case file – "Slater wrote in his statement that she was out with friends on Monday, and yet she is telling us she was on her own, shopping."

"Maybe she didn't want to tell him where she was going," Calderwood pointed out. "Slater said something about her spending too much money. Maybe he's a bit tight, and she wanted to avoid an argument. That doesn't make her a killer. And neither does calling you a horrible little man. She was upset."

"I think she is ruthless, and lying through her teeth," McCord said, "and her shock at Slater's affair could well be just a bit of acting. I'm sure she already saw herself as Mrs Slater on a yacht in the Caribbean. She could have got rid of her rival only to find out that Slater still didn't want her. We need to check her alibi for both Monday night and Thursday. Get Dharwan onto that. Oh, and ask her to check what car Dunbar drives. I don't trust Struthers to do the job properly."

McCord tapped the desk with his forefinger, deciding to ignore Calderwood's remark about that woman calling him little. Five foot ten was a respectable height for a man, and even if he did have certain sensitivities around that subject, he prided himself on never letting it influence his judgement. However, had McCord reflected on his reaction, he would have observed that being called horrible did not faze him at all.

"And what about that story with the child?" he said. "Weird. Would that woman make such a fuss if she didn't believe Slater was the father? She must know that she would be easily found out. It looks to me as if our Ms Dunbar is unwilling to accept the truth. No wonder Slater is worried about telling her about his affair and leaving her. I would be scared if I were him."

"So, you don't think Cartwright is our man anymore?" Calderwood said.

"He probably is," McCord said, "but I want her checked out, and there is no need to pussyfoot about just because her boyfriend has won the lottery. We need this accident out of the way. Until it is, we have two murderers on the loose."

Chapter 14

As Amy was following Amanda Jackson along Niddrie Mains Road in Craigmillar, she regretted asking her mum to cobble together a dark, loose garment for her after-tanning care. The black, floor-length kimono imprinted with pink cherry blossoms would have been fine for nipping back home in the car but, looking like somebody wandering around in her dressing gown, she drew far too much unwelcome attention from passers-by. Valerie had been slightly suspicious because Amy had so far shunned any expensive beauty treatments and even plucked her own eyebrows. She also could not see the need for an artificial tan when her daughter already had the most beautiful skin tone possible. But Amy had persuaded her that there were things in a girl's life that one just had to try, if only once.

When she passed a group of youths, one of them dog-whistled at her, and she dived into a sandwich shop, afraid Jackson might turn round. Amy wondered how long it would take Calderwood and McCord to get here. She had sent Calderwood a hurried text explaining the situation, while she was waiting at the salon, supposedly for her tan to dry, but really to hang around until Jackson had to leave. Calderwood had sent a question mark, but after her 'Please!!!', he'd replied with 'On our way'. So, he was bringing McCord. Good.

Amy stuck her head out into the street just in time to spot Jackson turning off into Harewood Drive. The time until the meeting was almost up, and Jackson hurried along, oblivious to her surroundings. Amy looked at the house numbers. Jackson's place had to be the third one along. Against the gate leaned a thuggish-looking male with tattoos up to his brutal chin. This was definitely not his neighbourhood. Amy could easily see him pushing Sarah Cartwright to her death for a couple of thousand quid.

In the absence of any cover, Amy dived behind a van two houses down and crawled forward, using the parked cars to shield her from view until she was level with the entrance.

Crouching down, she messaged Calderwood again. 'Deal about to happen, where are you?' Send.

Then she peeked through the windows of the van. The guy had pushed himself off the gate as Jackson approached him, and they were standing there, staring belligerently at each other.

"Finally," the guy said with a stony face. "Let's get this over with."

It took Jackson a while to unlock the front door. Her hands must be shaking, Amy thought. Then both of them disappeared inside.

* * *

"Tell me again why we are on a wee jaunt to Craigmillar when we are supposed to be finding out how Daniel Slater crashed his Porsche?" McCord asked as he and Calderwood were driving down Prestonfield Avenue as fast as the rush-hour traffic would allow.

"Because Amy is following a lead that we should have picked up," Calderwood said. "Amanda Jackson was Sarah Cartwright's best friend but claims she didn't know a thing about a lover and Sarah suddenly coming into money. She also failed to mention that she was Ross's girlfriend before he dumped her for Sarah. And now she's doing some sort of deal with a dodgy-sounding male."

"And Amy thinks she is bearing old grudges and has paid somebody to bump off her bestie?" McCord asked. "Silly idea. I think it's much more likely to be a drugs deal, and we'll end up with nothing but a pile of paperwork."

"And yet, you have agreed to come," Calderwood said.

"Only because I'm sick of you going on about me not taking Amy seriously."

"And because you're worried about her," Calderwood added.

McCord shrugged. "She has a talent for getting herself into a fix."

Calderwood's phone pinged. "They've gone inside Jackson's house. 38 Harewood Drive. From Niddrie Mains Road, second left."

"Tell her to wait outside. Not that she'll pay attention to anything I say."

"That sounds familiar," Calderwood said, holding on to the dashboard as McCord ignored a little Fiat's right of way and stepped on the accelerator.

* * *

Amy inched closer to the door that the guy had left slightly ajar. Pretty brazen of him, under the circumstances, but then, he didn't know that she was on their trail. Amy heard Jackson's angry voice.

"I told you you'd get it, there was no need to call me at work," she said.

"Four days I've been waiting," the guy said. "All I want is what's mine, and then I'm out of here, and you're rid of me for good."

Then Jackson again. "Can't wait!"

Amy heard a box being opened.

"It's all there," Jackson said.

Amy heard the sound of someone patting on cardboard.

"Always better to check," the guy said.

Amy jumped as McCord suddenly appeared at her shoulder.

"She's just handed over the money," Amy whispered.

McCord put a finger to his lips and gave Calderwood a sign. Both men were wearing bulletproof vests.

They made to storm the flat together, but the entrance was too narrow for them both, and they collided in the doorway. Amy could not suppress a giggle that earned her a death stare from McCord. Calderwood edged ahead and ran inside.

"Police!" he shouted.

Calderwood and McCord barged into the living room where Amanda Jackson and a young man stood rooted to the spot.

"Hands up!"

Calderwood swiftly patted down the young man. Jackson was wearing a clingy top over a miniskirt, and there was clearly no room anywhere to conceal a deadly weapon.

She was first to regain her wits.

"What are you doing here?" she asked McCord and Calderwood.

"You know them?" the young man asked.

"I went to the station to tell them about Ross Cartwright, you know?"

"Yeah, the dude who killed Sarah?"

At that point, Jackson noticed Amy sidling into the room.

"*You?* What did you call the police for? It was just a fake tan gone wrong, for chrissake, and I didn't even charge you!"

McCord looked perplexed at this exchange but pressed on regardless.

"Hand over the box!"

The young man reluctantly passed the box to McCord, who opened the flaps. "I want it back, mind, it's mine!"

"What the hell is this?" he asked Calderwood.

Calderwood examined the contents, his face inscrutable. "It seems to be a games console and computer games, sir."

McCord lifted his head and locked eyes with Amy.

"Is there a rational explanation for this?"

Hot tears of humiliation stung her eyes. Furious with herself, she turned on the young man.

"You threatened Mandy on the phone, and you said something about a deal! Who are you anyway?"

"Don't you dare speak to Darren like that," Jackson hissed. "He's done nothing wrong, and me neither!"

"We were informed that an illegal activity might be taking place on these premises," Calderwood intervened. "Could I please have your name?"

The young man turned to Jackson as if waiting for an answer why this was happening to him. "I'm Darren Pollock."

"And what are you doing here, Mr Pollock?"

He looked again at Jackson.

"I'm… I was Mandy's boyfriend. We broke up on Monday, and I told her I wanted my games console back."

"That's absolutely true," Jackson said, grasping his arm, "and you have no right to treat him like a criminal! Barging into innocent people's houses, like that. I think your superior officer should know–"

"We are only doing our job," McCord said weakly.

He had realised by now that they had no business to be here at all and dreaded to think what Hepburn would say if she found out about this.

But then Amy squared up to Jackson. "I think your boss would also be interested to hear what you've done to my legs," she said, flicking open her kimono.

Everybody gaped at her discoloured legs. Darren Pollock gave a low whistle.

"All this seems to have been an unfortunate misunderstanding," Calderwood said soothingly. "I think we've all made mistakes that we regret, haven't we?"

Jackson scowled at Amy. "I suppose so."

"Excellent. Can we give you a lift somewhere, Mr Pollock?" Calderwood asked.

Darren Pollock hesitated and faced Jackson.

"That was really cool how you stood up for me there with the police and all. I'm so sorry, babe, I broke up with you on the day your chum died. That was totally out of order. I should've been there for you."

"No, I'm sorry. I shouldn't have cut up your Hibs shirt. And, you know, I only kept the games 'cause I was hoping you'd come back for them, and we could…" She gave a coquettish shrug.

His face lit up. "Really, babe? You're going to give me another chance?"

Jackson nodded, in tears. "I love you, you numpty."

They flew into each other's arms and began to kiss passionately.

Calderwood gave McCord a look that said, 'See, that's how it's done.'

McCord grunted.

"We should be off. I don't think he needs a lift anymore."

Outside, McCord looked regretfully down the road towards Niddrie.

"My dad's just a mile away from here. It's our curry night, but I'll need to cancel because I'm investigating car accidents these days."

He turned to Amy. "I suppose you would like a lift back to the city?"

"No, thanks, I've got Mum's car round the corner." She swallowed. "I'm so, so sorry, McCord. If it's any consolation, I feel like a right idiot."

McCord looked at her long and hard without saying anything. Then his gaze dropped to her feet, where orange skin protruded between the straps of her sandals.

"And so you should. But at least the colour of your legs matches my office walls now."

McCord had barely had time to log onto his computer when Hepburn knocked perfunctorily on the half-open door.

"Ma'am," Calderwood said, rising swiftly from his chair.

McCord took a little longer.

"Where have you been?" she asked. "I wanted to check if there is an update on the car crash yet."

"It's only been a few hours," McCord said, ignoring her question. "We've interviewed Slater's girlfriend, who had motive if she knew about his affair, but she claims to have an alibi."

"And what about Cartwright? Surely, if he can prove he was elsewhere at the time…"

She didn't need to spell it out. Cartwright's alibi would not solve any case, but it would solve Hepburn's biggest PR problem to date.

"We are working on that," McCord said, trying to remain calm. "I'm going to speak to him tonight and see if he lets us have a look at his car. I suspect, though, that he has a lawyer now who will want to see a warrant."

"No problem, Russell," chirped Hepburn. "You know, I'm always happy to help. I'll get you any warrant you need, just say the word."

McCord felt he should show appreciation of the offer, but he was distracted by the agonising indecision over whether to call her Heppie or not to address her at all. The first option was physically painful, the second rude and, seeing that Calderwood needed protection from her, unwise. He remembered what it had felt like to almost lose his partner, so he did what had to be done. "Thank you, Heppie. By the way, it was DS Calderwood who drew my attention to Dunbar as a potential suspect."

Hepburn nodded to Calderwood and gave McCord a big smile as she finally turned to go, saying, "I'm so glad that we are such a good team!"

When she was safely out of earshot, Calderwood said, "Thank you, sir. You might want to be careful, though."

"I am being careful," McCord said. "I won't give her any excuse to drag you down."

"That's not what I meant," Calderwood said. "I mean that she's got a soft spot for you."

"A soft… that's ridiculous!"

"Risen to DI from humble beginnings, bravery award, dark and brooding, what's not to like?" Calderwood started to giggle.

McCord suppressed a rising panic.

"Ach, shut up!"

He picked up his jacket.

"Come on, let's see how hospitable our main suspect is."

Calderwood looked out of the dirty window. Through the streaks he could still make out the pale blue evening sky.

"Shall we walk? It's a nice night and his flat isn't far from here. We could grab a bite at the Kismot afterwards. Not quite the same thing as your curry night but better than nothing."

And once again, McCord thought how lucky he was to have Calderwood as his partner.

* * *

It was approaching eight o'clock by the time Calderwood rang the bell at Ross Cartwright's flat on Prestonfield Avenue. It took three more attempts, the length and urgency of the sound increasing each time, until they heard shuffling punctuated by muttering on the inside.

The lock was pushed back with some feeling, and then the hirsute face appeared in the gap between the door and the frame. With faint disgust, McCord noticed remnants of brown sauce on Cartwright's beard.

"What do youse want now?"

"So sorry to disturb you, Mr Cartwright," Calderwood said pleasantly. "We would like to ask you a few more questions if you don't mind."

"I bloody well do mind," Cartwright said. "I'm having me dinner, and I need to get ready for work."

"So soon after your wife's death?" McCord asked.

"It probably helps you to take your mind off things," Calderwood answered instead of Cartwright, whose growing anger subsided a little. "It won't take long. We have only a couple of questions for you."

"Me lawyer says not to speak to you unless he's there and not to let you in without a warrant. I didn't kill me wife, and that's all you need to know."

McCord was about to tell him that if he wanted to play it that way, they would continue the conversation under caution at the station, but Calderwood got in there first.

"We understand, Mr Cartwright, but this is not about your wife. We were hoping you could give us some information on a different matter, which might even help us to eliminate you from our inquiry into your wife's death."

Cartwright looked at them suspiciously but decided that asking a question could not do him any harm. "What's this about then?"

"Mr Daniel Slater, who you met yesterday, had a car accident soon after he left the station."

A glow of satisfaction spread across Cartwright's face. "Aye, I read about that in the papers."

"Did you happen to see whether anybody was following him when you left the car park?" Calderwood asked.

Cartwright frowned. "Hang on a minute. You're not trying to pin this on me as well? Me lawyer was right, I should've—"

"Please wait!" Calderwood almost shouted to stop him from closing the door. "If we could have a look at your car or you have an alibi, tell us, then we can eliminate you—"

The face receded and the door slammed shut.

"If you want anything else, contact me lawyer," Cartwright shouted from the inside.

McCord had had enough. He opened the flap in the door and spoke very slowly, enunciating every word.

"You contact your lawyer and tell him we want to speak to you tomorrow morning at the station. Either you come voluntarily to answer our questions, or we'll come and arrest you not only on a murder charge, but also one of attempted murder. We will also have a warrant by then, and we'll rip this place apart."

He let the flap fall with a clatter and turned to leave.

"Sorry," Calderwood said quietly to McCord as they were walking back to the car.

"You did well," McCord said. "For a moment I thought you had him there. Never mind, unless we find something pointing to the contrary, he's smack bang back in the frame."

Chapter 15

It was quarter to eleven on Saturday morning when Amy steered her mother's vintage MG into the ALDI car park on Oxgangs Road North. Her mind was not on bargains, however, but on hunting of another kind. After the previous day's fiasco, she had a lot to prove to McCord.

It had not taken her long to establish an online profile of Kimberley MacLean, who had not only posted spiteful comments about Daniel Slater and Yvonne Dunbar, but also cute pictures of her little boy at the local playgroup.

Oxgangs is one of those areas of Edinburgh where the wealthy and the hard-up live quietly in close proximity as if the poorer citizens didn't mind the yawning gap in their fortunes and the rich didn't care.

Amy crossed the road and walked towards Oxgangs Library, a modern, salmon-coloured building, which formed a cheerful contrast to the drab semis around it.

When Amy asked about the Bookbug group, the receptionist doubtfully glanced at Amy's high heels and elegant trouser suit.

"I'm here to see Kimberley and Riley," Amy said. "They are here, aren't they?"

"I'm not sure, I only started the job last week, but the session finishes at eleven if you want to wait?"

An out-of-tune rendition of *The Wheels on the Bus* sounded from the adjoining room, and by the fourth stanza, Amy felt that the song had indeed lasted all day long.

"Cute, isn't it?" The receptionist's remark was followed by a sigh indicating that she would rather be in there with a little tot of her own than sitting at her desk.

"Very cute."

Amy was not entirely sure how she felt about having kids. A warm, fuzzy feeling stirred in her chest whenever she walked past a baby sleeping peacefully in a pram, but when they were awake, the budding desire was swiftly extinguished and replaced by irritation.

Amy ostensibly studied the leaflets on the table but in truth was rehearsing the spiel that might entice Kimberley MacLean to share her grievances.

A few minutes later, there was a scraping of chairs and noisy chattering, and a group of women as well as a couple of men filed past her with babies and toddlers in car seats, prams and buggies. The women eyed Amy with either envy or pity, depending on how much they were enjoying motherhood at that moment, while the men found it difficult to take their eyes off her.

Amy put on a cheerful smile while she scanned the women's faces. As the line became thinner and eventually petered out, her heart sank. A wasted journey through the Edinburgh traffic. But then the sound of a howling toddler gave her renewed hope.

On one of the chairs inside the room sat Kimberley MacLean. Dressed in faded jeans – not the fashionable kind – and worn-out pumps, she was trying to calm the little boy sitting next to her by handing him simultaneously a wine gum and a tablet with a frayed cover. He grabbed the sweet with a grubby hand, shoved it in his mouth and immediately fixed his gaze on the screen, where a little blue dog was getting up to mischief. With the child oblivious to the outside world, the mother used the opportunity to wipe the snot off his face and then sank back into her seat with a sigh.

Amy walked towards her with a face she hoped expressed sympathy and sat down next to her.

"Hi, I'm Amy. What's the wee one's name?"

"Riley," Kimberley said proudly. "Are you waiting to be picked up as well?"

"No, actually, I was hoping to speak to you."

"Why?" MacLean asked suspiciously. "You're not from welfare, are you?"

Amy shook her head. "No, no, don't worry. I'm writing a series of articles about lottery winners, and one of them is about Daniel Slater."

"Ah." MacLean scrutinised Amy's face but said nothing more.

"I read your posts online and wondered if you would like to share your story with a wider audience."

"And what's in it for me?" MacLean asked.

"Somebody who listens to your grievances and might help you get what should be yours."

MacLean pondered this, and eventually held the open bag of wine gums out to Amy. When she politely declined,

MacLean fished one out for herself and popped it into her mouth.

"Dan is Riley's dad," she said, moving the glutinous red mass around her mouth so that every so often her teeth looked bloodstained. "But he's never paid a penny in child support, no birthday present, no Christmas present, nothing. If it weren't for my mum, me and Riley would be out on the street."

"That is shocking," Amy said, trying to marry this statement with the picture of the caring, modest guy Yvonne Dunbar had painted.

"But he's no getting away with that! He'll give my Riley what's due!"

"I'm sure he will," Amy said.

She looked at the boy. He was now completely engrossed in the gentle telling-off the little blue dog was receiving from his unquestionable father, whose calm reasoning would have been applauded by Education Scotland.

"I assume Dan has done a paternity test?" Amy asked.

MacLean pulled herself up.

"Are you calling me a liar?"

"No," Amy hastily replied, "all I meant was if there was a positive test, then the situation would be clear, and you would easily get your money."

"I tried to talk to him, but I didn't even get past his girlfriend. She was like a bloody guard dog. She said he didn't have to do a test, and it was a waste of time anyway because he wasn't the father. How would she know, eh? But I'm not having that. I've applied to the court, but you know what they've said? They can't make anybody take a DNA test against their will. Something to do with effing human rights. What about my rights, and Riley's rights, eh?"

"Surely, though, the courts must support children like Riley," Amy said. "They can't allow men to father children and then simply walk away."

"They told me, if Dan refused the test, the court would assume that he is the father and order him to pay. But that is going to take ages. I need the money now." MacLean's eyes lit up. "Are you going to pay me if I tell you the whole story?"

"*Forth Write* magazine is not that kind of paper," Amy said. "My boss would want to see proof before we print anything that could ruin somebody's reputation."

MacLean scowled. "Well, if you change your mind, you know how to find me."

She pulled out her buzzing phone and quickly typed a message.

"It's your granny," she said to Riley. "She's parked outside ALDI. We're going to get you something for lunch."

At the word 'lunch', the boy pricked up his ears, threw the tablet on the floor and clambered down from the seat.

"Lun-tch!" he bellowed.

"How many times have I told you not to throw the tablet about?" she shouted back at him.

Amy picked it up and handed it to MacLean.

"It's okay, the screen's not broken."

"Cheers," MacLean said with a relieved sigh.

She stowed the battered device and the bag of sweets away in her shoulder bag, lifted the child into the buggy and strapped him in. "Kids, eh? Who'd have them?"

And with that, she departed.

Chapter 16

At St Leonard's, Jack Carruthers phoned McCord's office to announce the arrival of Ross Cartwright and his lawyer, who was reputed to charge a small fortune for his services.

"Either he is not as hard-up as we thought, or he is desperate," McCord said. "Unless he is banking on the money that his wife got from Slater, which is also interesting."

The solicitor was a pleasant gent in his fifties who looked tired and slightly uncomfortable. This did not surprise McCord; he would not have wanted to be the one to defend Cartwright either. There might have been money in it, but glory there certainly was not.

According to the enduring newspaper interest, most people thought Cartwright was guilty as hell and wondered why he was still a free man. McCord guessed he was not the most cooperative client either.

He shook hands with the solicitor. He had met him before, and while he had no fondness for the species, he acknowledged its rightful place within a system based on law and order. This particular specimen was sensible and mild-mannered.

"Good morning, Mr Cartwright," McCord said. "I'm glad you saved us a trip in the car. We will bear that in mind as we proceed."

He ushered them into one of the interview rooms, where Calderwood was ready to start the recording.

Once they were all seated, McCord began.

"Mr Cartwright, as we speak, a forensics team is examining your car."

He pushed the warrant across the table to the solicitor, who picked it up, scanned it and nodded to Cartwright.

"Before I get their report, is there anything you want to share with us about Mr Slater's car crash?"

The solicitor nodded encouragingly towards his client.

"I left the station about the same time as Slater," Cartwright said. "He zoomed off in his Porsche, and I–" he looked to the solicitor for support "–just drove around for an hour or so and then I went home."

"You weren't tempted to follow Mr Slater after meeting him at the station?" asked McCord.

Cartwright looked at him as if he was stupid.

"My old banger could hardly keep up with a Porsche."

"So, where did you 'drive around'?" McCord asked.

"Dunno," Cartwright said. "Here and there."

"I'm afraid you need to be a little more specific," McCord said. "'Here and there' does not constitute a very good alibi."

Cartwright leaned forward. "I was upset, alright?"

"And angry?"

"Wouldn't you have been? He was screwing my wife!"

The solicitor held up his hand. "Mr Cartwright remembers driving on the A68 towards Jedburgh. A traffic camera might have picked him up."

"Problem is," McCord said, "the direct route to Jedburgh would have led Mr Cartwright along Old Dalkeith Road and past the scene of the accident. Did you see any signs of an accident on your way, Mr Cartwright?"

Cartwright shook his head. "I didn't go straight there. I've told you, I was driving around, I didn't care where I was going. I was meant to meet up with a mate, but I wasn't in the mood after that."

McCord closed his eyes. It was an unfamiliar situation for him, hoping for his prime suspect to present a watertight alibi. As much as he wanted Cartwright to go down for his wife's murder, he was almost equally keen to prove that he was not responsible for Slater's accident. Until that happened, the press would be going on about it, and Hepburn would be pestering him like an infestation of bedbugs.

"Let's go back to the weeks before your wife's murder," McCord said. "My officers have found witnesses who say that, more than once, you turned up at her workplace unannounced. Your wife also mentioned to others that you were checking up on her, and that your jealousy caused her considerable distress."

Cartwright's cheeks reddened under the untamed growth of the beard. "I didn't see any distress. She was happy, excited, 'cause she was about to go off with a ridiculously rich bloke!"

McCord sat up.

"So, you admit knowing about the affair before you met Mr Slater at the station?"

"That's not what Mr Cartwright was saying," the lawyer interjected, almost apologetically. "Please, don't put words into my client's mouth."

McCord ignored him. "You knew, right?"

"I didn't," Cartwright shouted. "Not then anyways, but I had a gut feeling that something was off. And I turned out to be right, didn't I?"

The solicitor cleared his throat. "I think it is important to stress here that Mr Cartwright adored his wife and was keen to save their marriage. At the time, he had no desire or reason to hurt her. His behaviour was certainly not wise, but it does not prove in any way that he was intent on harming, let alone killing her. Similarly, being angry with Mr Slater does not mean that he caused the car crash."

Cartwright sat up.

"I wouldn't have done it like that anyway. What I really wanted was to throttle—"

"You have no evidence whatsoever against my client, DI McCord. It seems to me that you are merely on a fishing expedition. I think we should stop the interview here," the solicitor said.

McCord suppressed a sigh. Although he hated to admit it, even to himself, he agreed with Cartwright that a car chase was not his style. Cartwright liked to get up close and personal, for example pushing a cheating wife off a cliff. But McCord saw no sign of Cartwright being about to crack, and still, they had not a shred of evidence against him.

"Please, try to remember any place you passed on your journey, so we can rule you out of our accident inquiry," McCord said. "Interview terminated at 10.18."

* * *

Back in his Sunset Boulevard, McCord found he had an unexpected visitor. There was something surreal about this strange bird of paradise fluttering about in the orange glow, but he knew Martin Eden to be Amy's most loyal friend and far from the fool he looked. The last time he had been in his office, he had alerted McCord to the fact that Amy was in serious danger.

"Please, have a seat, Mr Eden. Is Amy alright?"

"That depends on one's point of view, DI McCord," Martin answered. "She would tell you that she is perfectly fine, but I thought you should know that she has been on at least two dates with a man she met on Bumble. That's an online dating app," he added, correctly assuming that this was not part of McCord's world.

"Ah," McCord said, trying to keep the expression on his face neutral. "Is there any reason to be concerned about this man? Has he done anything illegal?"

"As far as I know, not yet," Martin conceded, "but as you well know, Amy is a very vulnerable young woman who could easily fall prey to a male predator."

McCord nodded, encouraging Martin to go on.

"She seems quite taken with this man but has so far declined to introduce him to her family, which is completely out of character and, you must admit, very suspicious."

Having met Valerie and been on the receiving end of her protectiveness towards her daughter, McCord thought this not surprising at all, but he played along with Martin's game.

"Until a crime has been committed, Mr Eden, I'm afraid I can't do anything about this," McCord said.

"Perhaps not in an official capacity," Martin said, rising. "But his name is Douglas, and he is a pastry chef in Edinburgh."

"Right," McCord said. "In such cases, the best plan is to keep communication lines open. I'm sure Amy will confide in you when things are getting serious."

McCord's mobile rang.

"Speak of the devil," McCord said, looking at the screen. "Hello, Amy."

Martin mimed a desperate plea not to tell her about his visit. McCord found it difficult to keep a straight face.

"Of course, I'm busy. Do you have something for me?"

"Nothing earth-shattering," Amy said, "but I've spoken to Kimberley MacLean. For what it's worth, I believe her. I also believe that she is desperate for money and would go to any lengths to get it."

"Thank you very much," McCord said with a glance at Martin who was nodding encouragingly. "I appreciate that. Is there anything you found that is beyond conjecture and actually of use to my investigation?"

Martin raised his outstretched arms to the heavens above.

Amy's angry voice even carried across to him. "MacLean doesn't have a car herself, but her mum does, and I've seen her getting into the driver's seat in the ALDI car park at Oxgangs. Happy now?"

McCord was about to give her some genuine praise, but she had already called off.

"I wish she wouldn't always hang up on me," McCord said. "It's so rude."

The office phone rang.

"DI McCord."

He gave Martin a wave goodbye.

"Don't leave it too late, DI McCord," Martin said and took off.

It was the leader of the forensics team on the phone. "Nothing definite yet, but so far, we haven't found anything to link Cartwright's car to the accident. There are a few scratches on it, but no paint matching the Porsche. Sorry."

"It's pretty much what I'd expected," McCord said. "You didn't find a map, by any chance, with a circle round the place where his wife was murdered?"

The woman at the other end of the line laughed. "Sadly not. If we do, you'll be the first to know."

McCord had barely put the phone down when Turner knocked on the door.

"I've got some background on Slater's half-brother, Richard McAllister. Do you want to hear about that now?"

"Anything that gets that car crash off our books," McCord said, pointing to the chair opposite his desk.

"Right," Turner said, straightening his tie, only to realise that he didn't have one on. "Sorry, sir."

Seeing that Turner had given up his weekend off as well, McCord was not about to be pedantic.

"Never mind. Do you think this Richard McAllister forced his brother off the road?"

"Not likely, in my opinion," Turner said. "When I spoke to him, I didn't get any sense that he hated or even disliked Slater. On the contrary, it was almost as if he felt that Slater had reason to dislike him."

"That's exactly what Miss Thornton told me," McCord said. "Did McAllister say why?"

"No, he was very cagey about that. He only said that they were just kids, and kids get it wrong sometimes."

"Hm. It must have been important, though, to cause such a rift."

"The brothers had a tough time of it," Turner said. "Daniel Slater is the older one, and his father bug— eh, abandoned him and his mother when he was a baby. The mother was then in a relationship with Richard's father, which seems to have been happy, but he died in a car accident. Drunk driver. Tragic. She never recovered, according to Richard. Drank very heavily; the boys were on the radar of social services, but they never really intervened until the mother died of a stroke when Daniel was fourteen and Richard twelve. They went into foster care, and Richard was eventually adopted by the McAllisters — a very nice couple by his account, who treated him like their own son. They sent him to Merchiston's, no less. It seems the school fees were not wasted. He did well there, and afterwards went to uni to study chemical engineering. He has a job, so it's not as if he desperately needs money."

"Nobody *needs* seven million pounds," McCord said, "but some people are willing to kill for that, and for much less. Please, tell me he has an alibi for Thursday lunchtime?"

"You're not going to like this, sir," Turner said. "Apparently, he was supposed to meet a colleague for lunch, but they cancelled, so because it was a nice day, he went out, bought a sandwich at Costa Coffee and sat on a bench in Princes Street Gardens." Before McCord could say anything, Turner hastily continued, "I asked. He didn't meet anybody he knew."

"Of course he didn't," McCord said, irritably flicking his pen on the edge of the desk, "and of course, it had to be a sunny day when everybody was milling around outside instead of staying inside and being clocked by people. You'll have to go to the M&S store and find me somebody, anybody, who remembers McAllister."

McCord was interrupted by a call on his mobile. As he was listening, his face lit up. "Thank you, we'll be there asap," he said and ended the call.

"Stand down, Turner, we're in luck. That was the Royal Infirmary. Slater is still dopey, but he has some lucid moments. No guarantees but we have permission to see him. Get Calderwood to drop everything and come here immediately. I only need a couple of words from Slater. 'No' or 'yes' and a name. Surely, he can manage that."

Chapter 17

At the ICU, McCord was surprised to be immediately recognised and warmly welcomed by the staff. It was five months since he had been treated here for a gunshot wound and achieved a certain celebrity status. The case of the missing diamonds seemed a lifetime away now, and rather than considering himself a hero, he felt inadequate and powerless. Two murders that might never be solved at this rate, and Amy was dating a chef. She was very partial to pastries, too. Hell.

As he and Calderwood were shown to Slater's bed, McCord fervently hoped that the young man would remember what happened on Old Dalkeith Road.

Yvonne Dunbar was sitting at the bedside, and her greeting was far less enthusiastic than that of the nurse.

"We're so glad that Mr Slater is getting better," Calderwood said with his disarming smile. "We need to ask him a couple of questions, and then we'll leave you two in peace."

Dunbar nodded like a queen graciously granting an unwelcome request.

"Alone," McCord said.

Dunbar gave him the death stare but faltered when she met his dark eyes.

"I'll be back in a minute, hon," she whispered.

McCord waited until she was out of earshot before turning to Slater. His head was bandaged, as was his left arm, which was connected to a drip. He had closed his eyes during Dunbar's departure but opened them again slowly when McCord pulled up a chair and leaned over him.

"Did somebody force you off the road?" McCord asked.

Slater frowned as if he was struggling to understand the question.

McCord decided to try again.

"Was somebody else there when you crashed?"

Slater opened his mouth but shut it again without saying anything. His eyes darted to the door.

McCord followed his gaze. The nurse was standing by the door with Dunbar, who was watching them, and a thought occurred to him.

"Do you feel safe with your girlfriend around?" he whispered.

Slater closed his eyes, and the steady bleeps of his heartbeat became fast. McCord was about to ask him again, but the nurse moved towards them.

"I'm sorry, but I must ask you to leave," she said. "Mr Slater needs to rest." She checked the monitor he was hooked up to, frowned and adjusted the drip.

McCord looked at Slater, but his eyes were still closed.

Dunbar all but pushed McCord to the side and sat down in her rightful place. She grasped Slater's hand, more possessive than tender, and McCord thought he saw him wince.

Outside in the corridor, McCord waited for the nurse to return.

"We are treating Mr Slater's accident as attempted murder," McCord said quietly. "We'll be sending an officer to guard him."

He glanced towards Slater and saw Dunbar looking at them through the open door. He backed further down the corridor, coaxing the nurse out of Dunbar's line of vision. "And keep a very close eye on the girlfriend," he added, almost in a whisper.

The nurse's eyes widened.

"Just in case."

McCord turned to go, leaving her staring after them.

* * *

"So, you agree with Amy, then," Calderwood said as they were walking towards the exit.

McCord grunted. "I wouldn't go that far. But it is too much of a coincidence, and Slater seemed very nervous to me, especially when I mentioned the girlfriend."

"No wonder," Calderwood said. "I think he realised that you told Dunbar about the affair. I would hate to be in his position."

McCord shrugged.

"I had to ask. And anyway, you would never be in his position because you wouldn't cheat on your girlfriend."

"None of us is infallible," Calderwood said with a hint of reproach. "Relationships are often complicated."

McCord was about to tell Calderwood to stop patronising him, but deep down he knew that his partner was right. Despite being younger as well as a posh git, Calderwood was by far the wiser of the two men, and McCord was both disturbed and reassured by the fact that, with the exception of his dad, Calderwood knew him better than anybody else in the world.

"At least Slater knows now that we're looking out for him," McCord said. "I'll send Turner and Dharwan to watch over him. I can hardly spare her at the station, but I need someone with a bit of nous here, not some dozy devil who falls asleep on the job."

Seeing Calderwood's face, he added, "Absence makes the heart grow fonder, or so I'm told. It'll dampen down the gossip going round the station if the two of you are not always seen flirting."

Calderwood bristled. "We are not! We've been extremely discreet!"

"So you have," McCord said with a smile. "But it's still very obvious that you are crazy about each other, even to me. As soon as we are back, get Dharwan into my office. I want to speak to her."

* * *

About twenty minutes later, Dharwan entered McCord's office. There was no outward sign that the summons had caused even a ripple of worry in her tranquil mood.

"How far did you get with Yvonne Dunbar's alibi?" McCord asked.

"I've been to all the shops Dunbar mentioned in her statement, but nobody remembers her browsing. She only bought a box of chocolates at M&S, she said, but didn't keep the receipt. The shop would have been still busy at that time, so no wonder the cashiers didn't notice her. Some of the shops have CCTV, but it'll take a while to go through it all."

"Get somebody else onto that," McCord said. "Until we have confirmation to the contrary, she has no alibi for Sarah Cartwright's murder. You find out how long it took her to get to the hospital after they called her about Slater's accident. She told us she was at home when she heard. Where do they live again?"

"Eskbank," Dharwan said. "That's only a few minutes down the road from where he crashed. She could have waited for him, forced him off the road, driven home and simply waited for the phone call from the police." She paused and frowned. "But this only makes sense if she knew about the affair and could guess when he was likely to be passing the accident spot. To prove she did it, we would need to catch her on CCTV coming from the scene of the accident."

McCord regarded her with an approving smile.

"Have you thought about going for promotion?" he asked.

Dharwan sat very straight.

"Isn't it too soon? I've been here less than two years."

"But we both know that you are ready, don't we?" It was a statement rather than a question.

"If you think so, sir," Dharwan said calmly, but McCord sensed the quiver of excitement that went through her.

"Good," he said. "Ask Calderwood if he has kept his textbooks, and I'm sure he'll be happy to coach you. But right now, I want you to go to the Infirmary. Keep an eye on Slater and Dunbar until we know what's going on there. The last thing I need is Slater dying on us now – although it would have the advantage of giving Hepburn a heart attack."

Dharwan laughed only with her eyes.

"There is one more thing," McCord said, serious again. "Relationships between officers, especially when they are of different ranks, are frowned upon."

Seeing Dharwan's mortified expression, he hastily continued, "Your behaviour is always above reproach. But I want you to know that I have spoken to Calderwood about this, too."

For the first time ever, McCord saw her flustered.

"I'm sure there was no need, sir. Duncan has always behaved like a gentleman."

"I'm sure he has," McCord said. "But there are people out there who are waiting for an opportunity to cause trouble for both of you. Let's not given them any ammunition."

Dharwan nodded solemnly.

McCord rose to accompany her back into the open-plan office where he stopped at Turner's desk. "I've put you on guard duty at Edinburgh Royal Infirmary."

"Oh no!" Turner clapped a hand over his mouth.

"Do you have a problem with that, Turner?" McCord asked sternly.

The young man hung his head. "No, sir, of course not. It's just…"

"What?" A tiny smile played on McCord's lips because he already knew the answer.

"Guard duty is so boring," Turner said.

"Allow me to explain," McCord said. "We think somebody tried to kill Daniel Slater. One of the suspects is Ross Cartwright, who probably pushed his wife down the Salisbury Crags out of jealousy and would love to do the same to her lover. Another suspect is Slater's possessive and greedy girlfriend who knows that he had an affair and that he might ditch her when he wakes up, which would put an end to the high life for her. I want Slater alive and well when we finally nail one of them, and I am relying on you and Dharwan to keep him safe. Is that exciting enough for you, Turner?"

Turner looked up.

"Of course, sir. Sorry, sir."

"Off you go, and get some sleep before your night shift."

Turner did not need to be told twice.

On his way back to the office, McCord stopped to ponder the incident board. Right next to the one showing all the known connections in the Sarah Cartwright murder, Calderwood had created a second incident board with Daniel Slater in the centre. A thick line connected him to Ross Cartwright, and radiating outwards were pictures of Yvonne Dunbar, Kimberley MacLean and Richard

McAllister. 7.8 million pounds. McCord tried to imagine what he would do with such a fortune. First, buy a three-bedroom flat in Musselburgh overlooking the Firth of Forth for himself and a bungalow for his dad and Clare, his dad's fiancée.

This thought reminded him of the embossed card that had been sitting at home on his mantlepiece for a couple of weeks now. He suspected the physical discomfort it was giving him could be the beginning of his very own stomach ulcer. The card requested the pleasure of his company at their wedding at Dalhousie Castle on 22 September. It would be a small, intimate affair, his dad had said, only family and a few good friends, which was exactly what McCord had hoped for.

When asked, however, what they would like as a present, his dad had told him that all he and Clare wanted was for him to bring Amy along as his 'plus-one'. Keith and Clare had met Amy briefly, but never got to know her properly. Straight after the outing to the Isle of May, McCord had been all geared up to asking her, but then Amy had suddenly gone all funny. And now that she was dating this blasted pastry chef, he could hardly ask her to be his plus-one. Or could he? Martin Eden seemed to think that he should do something, but he was not even sure what 'plus-one' meant. Did it imply that you were in a relationship? Then it would be far too presumptuous. He decided to ask Calderwood later. But first, he needed to crack this case.

He looked again at the board. 7.8 million pounds. That amount of money had to be at the heart of the problem. Such a sum made people envious and greedy, and possibly even turned them into murderers.

The question was simple: who would have benefited from Daniel Slater's death? First, his son, if he was his, and indirectly Kimberley McLean. He had to get her in for a chat, if only to eliminate her. And as soon as Slater was able to give consent, he'd encourage him to do a paternity test. What about Yvonne Dunbar? If Slater hadn't made a will, she would not get a penny, and if the boy wasn't his, his next of kin would be… Richard McAllister. His sudden interest in his brother's well-being was more than suspicious. He needed to ask Slater if he had made a will; maybe there were other people who would inherit.

McCord went over to Struthers' workstation.

"Any progress with the cars of our suspects?"

Struthers cleared his throat.

"Cartwright drives a white Ford Escort, as we already knew, Dunbar a teal Aston Martin. Kimberley MacLean has a driving licence, but no car is registered to her."

He looked expectantly at McCord, but the expected praise was not forthcoming.

"Check her mother's car. Apparently, MacLean uses that on occasion. Were any of the others in the vicinity when Slater's car crashed?"

"The traffic cameras are few and far between, and there is no CCTV near the accident site, so I haven't…"

The sentence petered out.

"Well, get the footage from the nearest camera you can find and start with Ross Cartwright's car."

Struthers sighed. "But—"

McCord was sorely tempted to kick his chair and send him flying across the office. Instead, he looked sternly at the DS and said, "Listen, Struthers, when I tell you to do something, you do it quickly and thoroughly. You are always the first to complain about others; why don't you stop whinging and just get on with it?"

Struthers turned back to his screen with a scowl. McCord now noticed the other officers observing the scene with some glee, and one look from him sent them back to their tasks.

He walked across to Sutton's den and knocked. Having been admitted by a croaky "come in", he wound his way to the inner sanctum.

"I need you to look into the accounts of Daniel Slater and Yvonne Dunbar again."

"What for?" she asked.

"I don't know," he admitted. "Just a feeling about her. Too pink and fluffy."

Sutton stared uncomprehendingly at his chin.

"You haven't met her," he said. "By the way, DCI Hepburn wants to do your appraisal."

Sutton's pallid face contorted in utter panic, and she shook her head violently.

"You'll be fine," McCord said. "DCI Hepburn prides herself on being supportive, especially…" He swallowed the rest of the sentence. Sutton's head was still swaying so manically that McCord began to worry that she might injure herself. "How about me going through the questions with you? We can figure out the answers together, and then you practise them?"

Sutton still looked as if she had been asked to hold a speech in parliament, but at least her head had come to rest.

"It'll be difficult, but you can do this," McCord said. "Nothing bad is going to happen. If they transfer you, it'll be over my dead body."

McCord thought he saw tears glisten under Sutton's twitching eyelids as she returned to her keyboard.

Coughing away a frog in his throat, he backed out of the den.

Chapter 18

McCord's hopes of being able to get on with the investigation into Sarah Cartwright's and Jai Sandhu's murders during the weekend were shattered when Hepburn turned up unexpectedly at the station. Even though she was off duty, she was wearing her obligatory trouser suit.

"I've had word from the STV team," she told McCord. "The re-enactment of the Sandhu killing is done, and the programme is going to be aired on Tuesday. Are we any closer to a definite answer why Daniel Slater crashed?"

"Not really, no."

"I do appreciate everything you're doing," Hepburn said, "but are you saying that you've made no progress since yesterday?" Without waiting for an answer, she added, "We need to be more proactive."

McCord hated that word. Like all management speak, it was nothing but waffle obscuring a simple concept: doing your job.

Hepburn waited patiently for suggestions, but they were not forthcoming; McCord felt he was already doing all he could. Eventually, she sighed.

"I think I'll have to hold a press conference tomorrow lunchtime appealing for witnesses to the accident," she said. "If somebody comes forward, we can hopefully close this matter; if not, at least we'll be seen to be doing something. God, I hate them!" She burst out laughing. "The press conferences, I mean, not the witnesses."

McCord managed a smile, which she took as a sign of encouragement.

"It's one of the downsides of a promoted post," she said. "The vultures from the press are always out to get you. Police-bashing sells copies. And if you are unfortunate enough to be a woman… One wrong word, and they make you a target. Then you might as well resign."

"Yes… Ehm," McCord said. "So, where is it?"

"Where is what?" Hepburn asked absent-mindedly, lost in her PR anxieties.

"The video of the re-enactment and the interviews," McCord said, swallowing the 'of course'. "We need to check them for accuracy before they are broadcast, don't we?"

"Good thinking. You're right, one can't be too careful," Hepburn said. "I'll email you the link now. I'm afraid, one of my tyres has a slow puncture, and I need to get it fixed. I'm so grateful that you and your team are sacrificing your weekend off. What would I do without you?"

McCord could think of no answer to that.

"Good luck with the car," he said gruffly before Hepburn mercifully disappeared.

* * *

McCord had called Calderwood over to watch the video with him.

Despite the warm orange glow diffused by the office walls, a sudden chill descended on the two men as they watched a hooded figure, carrying a sports bag and a long stick, turn the corner onto Leith Walk. The narrator was telling the audience that it was five minutes after two o'clock in the morning and that Jai Sandhu was sleeping peacefully in his bed. How they knew this, McCord could not fathom, but even if uncorroborated, it made for better telly. The man on the screen looked around and pulled out a spray can.

The indignant voice went on to say that the perpetrator had used Black Matt All Purpose Aerosol Spray Paint to write his hateful message on the wall next to the entrance of the shop. A picture of a can of the same spray filled the screen. Since it was a common brand, readily available to any budding graffiti artist for a few pounds, McCord doubted that this information would lead to the apprehension of the killer, but they were in no position to be choosy.

The arsonist then lifted a petrol canister out of the bag and poured all its contents through the letter box.

The viewers were informed that the forensics team had used chromatography–mass spectrometry to determine that petrol had been used in the attack, which was not surprising since it had a much lower flashpoint than diesel, for example. One had to be very careful, the narrator explained, because there was a high risk of the arsonist getting burnt themselves. That is why the suspect had brought a long wooden torch, which he ignited and pushed as far into the letter box as possible.

"Great," McCord muttered, "just tell everybody out there how to commit arson without even getting your fringe singed."

Suddenly, the screen lit up with an explosion, and one could see the fire spreading through the shop downstairs; within a few minutes, the flat above was ablaze as well.

McCord recoiled.

"Wow! How did they do that? Surely they didn't blow up the burnt-out shop again?"

"It's amazing what they can do with computer graphics," Calderwood said, who had not flinched. "Look, there he goes."

The arsonist grabbed his bag, shoved the canister and can back inside and ran away in the same direction he had come from.

McCord stopped the recording. Something was stirring in the area of his brain where splinters of memories are stored, usually never to be revived. But what could it possibly have been? The image was far too blurred to identify the person and McCord hadn't been anywhere near the area where the attack had taken place. But there was this nagging feeling that something wasn't quite right.

Unable to capture it, he pressed play again. A picture of Sandhu's smiley face filled the screen. A mournful cello provided the soundtrack to the voice-over, which gave a summary of his blameless life. This was followed by interviews with his tearful sisters and Dharwan, who sounded both genuine and extremely competent. Calderwood drank in every second of her appearance, and McCord could not help smiling on seeing his partner's pride. Then it was McCord's turn, who was surprised to have come across rather well as Edinburgh's fierce pursuer of all wrongdoing.

"Nice shirt," Calderwood commented, and although McCord pretended to be above such considerations, he was secretly pleased.

The video ended with Hepburn urging the public to support her dedicated officers in solving this heinous crime. The tremor in her voice could have stemmed from anguish about the tragedy, but McCord knew better.

"I suppose that's as good as it could be," Calderwood said. "After all, we had very little to give them."

McCord was quiet.

"You alright, sir?" Calderwood asked. "I know, it's awful. By all accounts, Sandhu was such a nice guy. Surina was quite affected by the whole case."

"It doesn't make sense," McCord said, more to himself than his partner.

"Such murders never do," Calderwood said, "all we can do is—"

"That's not what I mean. Why did the killer spray the message before he set the place on fire? They ran a huge risk of being seen there, overlooked by I don't know how many windows. If it was a random racist attack, why not choose a more secluded location? And why Sandhu? If they wanted to make a point about immigration and so on, why choose somebody who was more of a Scot than you and me?"

Calderwood shrugged. "You said earlier that the killer can't have known Sandhu at all, or he wouldn't have confused him with a Pakistani."

"But that's exactly my point," McCord said. "We didn't find any link to our known racist thugs in the area, so what if the attack was not randomly racist at all, but personal? And the killer only left the message to make us think that it was racist?"

"But who would want to kill Sandhu?" Calderwood asked. "I'm sorry, but I don't buy your theory that Sarah Cartwright and Sandhu had an affair. And Surina excluded Ross as a suspect, because of his build. We couldn't find a motive anywhere in the family or among his friends. Everybody loved him."

"And yet, he is dead," McCord said. "So, if he didn't harm anybody, why did he have to die?"

"Maybe he knew something?" Calderwood suggested.

McCord's eyes lit up.

"Yes! All day, every day in his shop, he would have seen people and overheard their talk. Maybe he saw or heard something that he shouldn't have. And who do we know went to his shop and also met a violent end?"

"Sarah Cartwright!" Calderwood exclaimed. "But what could he have found out about her that led to his death? You don't think that Sarah Cartwright killed him and was then murdered herself?"

"I don't know," McCord said. "The height is about right, but she was very slim." He rewound the video to the point where the figure stood upright. "It's difficult to tell with the hoodie and the jacket."

He leant back in his chair. "It seems far-fetched, but we need to remember that we know very little about Sarah

Cartwright. She had a secret lover and a secret stash of money – who knows what other secrets she kept?"

"Maybe we should ask Amanda Jackson? We never mentioned Sandhu when she was here."

McCord was sceptical. "She didn't even know about the love affair and the money, but I suppose, we've got to try everything. Also, see if there is any way we can find out where she was during Sandhu's murder. You don't happen to remember an empty petrol can in her wardrobe?"

Calderwood shook his head and laughed. "Somehow, I don't think it'll be as easy as that."

* * *

That evening, Amy entered The Green Room wine bar in William Street. Richard McAllister had suggested the venue, and she was surprised. She had thought that he would choose something showy and shiny, but not something like this. The medieval stone was painted dark green and provided a strong contrast to the colourful flowers in the hanging baskets on either side of the door. The wrought-iron lamps shed a warm light onto the damp pavement. It was another dull evening; after the June heatwave, July had been cool and wet, which reminded the residents why they had dreamed of a holiday abroad all the way through the dark winter months.

Inside, it was cosy, and conversations were muted. As her eyes adjusted to the dim light, she saw McAllister wave to her from a small corner table. She was not sure what he expected from this meeting. Was it genuine concern about his brother or was he simply going to hit on her? He certainly had turned on the charm when she had contacted him first. Either way, she was curious, and the idea of bringing together two estranged brothers did appeal to her. Daniel Slater's world had spectacularly imploded since his lottery win, and if she could repair at least one aspect of his broken life, she would gladly do it, especially if there was a good story behind it.

McAllister rose from his chair and waited politely for her to take off her raincoat and hang it on a hook on the wall. He had already secured the menus, and after a brief discussion with the waiter on the merits of French as opposed to New World wines, he ordered a board of cold meats and cheese to go with his merlot, while Amy chose smoked salmon and, considering the price tag, a glass of Chilian chardonnay.

"You are my guest, of course," McAllister said lightly. "I'm very grateful you called."

"Have you spoken to Dan yet?" Amy asked, hoping not to touch a sore point too soon in the evening.

McAllister shook his head.

"I went to the hospital this afternoon but was not allowed in."

"He is still very unwell," she said.

McAllister acknowledged her attempt to console him with a slight nod. "I hope the police are taking this seriously."

"Oh, I have no doubt about that. Dan has been so incredibly unlucky. This lottery win has been like a curse. First his lover is murdered, and then he is almost killed himself; the only question is, who it was – the jealous husband, his jealous girlfriend or this other woman who claims her child is his?"

McAllister sighed. "It just shows you how little I know about my big brother. I'd never thought he'd be the type. He used to be quite shy around girls. But then, we were only kids."

The waiter appeared and they silently watched him put down the wooden boards and their drinks.

"That looks delicious," Amy said, squeezing a lemon wedge over the salmon.

"Enjoy," McAllister said, tearing a bit off the baguette that had come with his meal and draping a paper-thin slice of dried ham over it.

"What do you actually do?" Amy asked, wanting to make polite conversation before delving into more personal matters.

"I work in my father's company," he said. "Oil and gas exploration. He is my adoptive father, as you probably know, but I could not have had a better one."

"That is nice," Amy said. "I gather your brother wasn't quite so lucky."

"Sadly, not," McAllister said. "Dan went to other foster parents. I'm sure they were good to him, though. The vetting process is very thorough, and we had a great social worker. He really seemed to care."

"I'm surprised you and Dan were not fostered together. One would have thought–"

McAllister cut a chunk of cheese with such force that the knife slid off the board.

"Everybody tried their best, but it didn't work out."

"I'm sure," Amy said hastily. "It was not meant as a criticism either of you or your parents."

McAllister smiled. "No offence taken."

"So, how come you and Dan lost touch?" Amy asked although she thought she knew the answer.

"Dan was very jealous of me. He thought it was incredibly unfair that I got adopted and he didn't. At first, he was sure that he would find a family as well, but unfortunately, it didn't happen. I tried to keep in touch and a few times bought him presents, stuff he couldn't afford, but he wanted nothing to do with me. Eventually, I gave up. Maybe I shouldn't have, but I was only a child then myself."

"And you thought now that he is far richer than your parents, he might be prepared to forgive you?"

McAllister nodded.

"And I was concerned about his accident. But when the police interviewed me, they seemed to think that I could have had something to do with it. Absurd, isn't it?

The thing is, I don't have an alibi. So I hope they find out soon who it was."

"I'm sure it won't take long. DI McCord is a pain—" she saw McAllister's shocked face and began to laugh "—but he is a very good detective… And a decent guy."

"I've read some of your articles," McAllister said. "It's amazing how you solved those cases together. I always thought…" He broke off.

"What?" Amy asked tetchily, spearing a piece of pink, juicy fish.

"I'm sure most of your readers think that you two have a wee thing going."

"We don't," Amy said, and her tone put an end to that topic of conversation.

McAllister was too well brought up to probe any further. "Another glass of chardonnay?"

"Only if you tell me what the terrible thing is that you did to your brother," Amy said, hoping that her light-hearted tone would make him confess.

"No way," McAllister replied. "Now that I've got you here, I'm not going to spoil it all by revealing what a nasty little brat I was then. Maybe on our second date."

His tone was flirtatious, but Amy sensed the shutters coming down. It had been too soon for confidences.

"Maybe," she said.

"I'd much rather hear about your travels in Europe. I went to Madrid with my parents when I was sixteen. Isn't it an amazing city?"

Chapter 19

The next morning, Daniel Slater looked a lot better. His face had lost its deathly pallor, and the bandage around his head had been replaced by a large plaster. At the sound of McCord and Calderwood approaching, he turned his face towards them. Yvonne Dunbar sat at his bedside; after smiling at Calderwood, she greeted McCord rather coolly.

"Good to see that you're recovering, Mr Slater," McCord said. "Could we have a word in private?"

Dunbar rose reluctantly but followed Calderwood outside. He found a way to be complimentary about her outfit and remarked it would have done nicely for the red carpet at Cannes.

McCord waited until Calderwood was back and ready with his notebook.

"Now that you're better, do you remember anything else about the accident? Was there another car? Can you remember the make? Colour? Size? A white Ford Escort, perhaps?"

Slater took a moment to process this. "Sorry. I have a feeling that there was something," he said. "I've been trying to remember, but I can't."

He waved his arms in frustration but winced and let them drop back onto the cover. "The doctor says temporary amnesia is normal and that my memory should come back. I hope she is right."

McCord sighed. "That's a great pity. Has Ms Dunbar talked to you about Sarah Cartwright?"

Slater made a futile attempt to lift his upper body. "Yvonne knows?"

"Do you not remember our last conversation?" McCord asked.

"Sort of, but I dream a lot, and sometimes I'm not sure what's real and what isn't."

"Yes, we had to ask her about the affair, but she said she didn't know anything about it, and she didn't believe me."

Slater groaned. "Oh God."

"She hasn't mentioned it at all?" McCord asked.

"No… but she's been acting weird. I thought it was because I almost died."

"Would you like me to keep her away from you?" McCord said. "I can arrange that."

Slater flung up his hands but gasped in pain when he pulled on the infusion.

"No, no, that would make it all worse. I'll have to come clean about Sarah. Maybe she'll be less angry because of the accident."

McCord thought Slater was being optimistic but did not comment.

"And what about the child?"

Slater stared at McCord. "What child?"

"The child Kimberley MacLean claims is yours. Is that true?"

"Oh, that. It was a one-night stand," Slater said. "I was single at the time, and she was on a break from her boyfriend. The kid's not mine; she never said anything afterwards about being pregnant. She must have heard that I've come into money."

"If you agreed to a paternity test, we could at least get the matter of the child resolved," McCord said. "If the child is not yours, Ms MacLean won't bother you further."

"But what if it's true?" Slater whispered. "A child?"

"I'm sure you can afford the maintenance now," McCord said drily.

"What about Yvonne? She won't want anything to do with the child."

"I thought you were planning on leaving her anyway?" McCord said. "Or have you changed your mind now that Sarah Cartwright is dead?"

Slater shook his head. "I'm struggling to take it all in. It's like a nightmare I can't wake up from."

"Okay, we're going to leave you in peace now, but one last thing," McCord said. "Have you made a will?"

"No," Slater said, "I didn't expect…"

"To die?" McCord shook his head. "It sometimes happens sooner than we think. I suppose you might as well wait until the paternity claim is resolved. If the boy is yours, he has the same right to inherit as a legitimate child would have."

"What a mess." Slater slumped back onto the pillow and closed his eyes.

"It's been a lot for you to take in," Calderwood said soothingly. "But it'll all work out in the end."

Slater opened his eyes and nodded weakly. "I hope so," he whispered.

"One other thing," McCord said, remembering what Amy had told him. "Have you spoken to your brother yet?"

Slater's face contorted. "Ricky? No, I haven't."

"He is very concerned about your well-being," McCord said.

"I don't want to see him."

The smooth waves on the monitor turned into a storm.

"Any particular reason?" McCord asked.

Slater began to shift in the bed. "I'm not feeling well. I need to rest."

"Don't worry," Calderwood said soothingly. "There'll be an officer at the door round the clock."

Slater quickly turned his head. "Why?"

"For your protection," McCord said, exchanging a concerned look with Calderwood. "It's possible somebody tried to kill you, Mr Slater. If that's the case, they might try again."

"Oh God." Slater closed his eyes again.

The detectives stood up.

"You have a good rest now, Mr Slater," Calderwood said. "I hope you feel better soon."

* * *

On the way back to St Leonard's, McCord presented his wedding invitation dilemma to Calderwood, who sat quietly while he was thinking it over.

"Amy is dating a pastry chef?" he asked eventually.

"That's what I've just told you. Gee, Calderwood, no wonder we haven't caught these killers yet if you're so slow on the uptake."

"She never mentioned it to me," Calderwood said, frowning. "And she told you?"

"Of course not. I have no idea what goes on in that woman's head," McCord said. "No, it was our little matchmaker, Martin Eden. I think he expects me to track down this guy Douglas and arrest him."

"Because he has broken the law, or because he dared to date Amy?"

"If you dig deep enough, you always find something," McCord said darkly. "Unfortunately, we're busy with real-life crime."

"There might be another possibility," Calderwood said.

"Which is?"

"A crazy suggestion: you tell Amy how you really feel."

McCord snorted. "Don't be ridiculous. She couldn't get away from me fast enough after the Isle of May. And that was when I thought things were going well. If it's a good-looking, fun guy who can make Danish pastry she's after, good luck to her."

Calderwood sighed.

"Anyway, that's not the question," McCord went on. "The question is if I should ask her to be my plus-one to keep my dad happy, or spare myself the inevitable humiliation. It's a choice between the devil and the deep blue sea."

"Of course, you should ask her," Calderwood said, exasperated.

"But even if she doesn't read anything into it and says 'yes', my dad will watch us like a hawk, expecting me to play lover boy to her. How am I supposed to do that? Damn, I've missed the turn-off!"

Uttering obscenities, McCord pulled into a side street, reversed into a drive and headed back up to the junction.

"Just ask her," Calderwood implored him. "And at the wedding, say something nice about her dress, have a few drinks and dance with her as much as possible. That'll please your dad, and nothing can go wrong."

McCord rejoined the main road.

"Calderwood, you have no idea how much can go wrong."

Chapter 20

When McCord and Calderwood arrived back at St Leonard's, a gaggle of reporters had assembled at the front door.

"Any progress on the Cartwright case, DI McCord?" somebody shouted.

A huge, furry microphone was shoved into his face.

"Detective Chief Inspector Hepburn is about to make an appeal for witnesses to Daniel Slater's car accident. You can ask her questions afterwards," McCord said, ploughing his way through the throng.

Inside, Hepburn was pacing up and down the corridor.

"Ah, there you are, Duncan. I still need my notes. We can't keep the members of the press waiting any longer. It's important that the appeal goes out for the lunchtime news."

Important to you, McCord thought.

Calderwood ran off to fetch the notes.

"Have you spoken to Daniel Slater?" Hepburn asked.

"That's where we've just been," McCord said.

"And? Please don't make me drag every single word out of you, Russell. My nerves are in shreds as it is."

"He couldn't give us any details about the crash, but he isn't quite with it yet. He might remember more when he is better."

"That's no use to me now," Hepburn said, wiping off the sweat forming on her upper lip. She pointed outside to the growing crowd. "They'll be asking me about the Cartwright case as well. Please tell me there is something positive I can say?"

"Ross Cartwright looks to be our man," McCord said, "but Mr Slater's girlfriend has motive, too, and her alibi is pretty vague."

"But we are getting somewhere, are we?" Hepburn asked.

We are getting nowhere, McCord thought, but said, "We are making progress… albeit slowly."

To his relief, Calderwood turned the corner and rushed towards them.

"Your notes, ma'am," he gasped.

"Well then," Hepburn said, drawing a deep breath, "time to face the enemy. Russell, why don't you join me? The public likes their heroes."

McCord shook his head.

"DS Calderwood is a lot more attractive. People always respond very well to him," he said pointedly.

"Alright," Hepburn said, clearly disappointed. "Let's do this."

"What did she say?!"

McCord banged his fist on the desk.

"She said that an arrest in the Cartwright case was imminent," Calderwood repeated.

"And what did you say?"

Calderwood blushed. "I could hardly contradict the DCI in front of the cameras, could I?"

"We'll have the hacks camping outside now waiting for us to drag somebody in. Shame we have nobody we can charge with anything. And then I'll never be done playing Hepburn's agony aunt!"

"The guys must be through the CCTV by now," Calderwood said. "I'll get onto them again. It is odd, though, that Dunbar hasn't spoken to Slater about the affair or the child. Maybe she wants to wait until he is better, or avoid a confrontation altogether. Even if she got rid of her rival, she can't afford to antagonise Slater too much. I think she might be playing the long game."

"Agreed," McCord said. "Kimberley MacLean was supposed to be in for a chat fifteen minutes ago, too, but she's late. Bring me back a cheese sandwich from the canteen when you go for lunch, will you?"

"Sure," Calderwood replied.

He was barely out of the door when Carruthers phoned to announce that a Ms Kimberley MacLean was on her way up.

"About time," McCord grumbled.

He positioned himself in the door frame. Unlike Yvonne Dunbar, Kimberley MacLean made no heads turn, although she looked pretty and had clearly smartened up for her visit to the station. Her hair was pinned up into a loose bun, and she was wearing tights under a flowing dress that accentuated her curves. The colour of the fake designer handbag matched her shoes, and the heels made a clacking sound.

McCord introduced himself and invited her to sit.

"Sorry I'm late," MacLean said. "My mum was supposed to babysit Riley, but she was held up. The traffic in the city centre was murder."

Feeling she'd led him neatly to the topic he wanted to discuss, he skipped the small talk.

"So, tell me why you turned up at Mr Slater's house and threatened his partner."

"Threatened?" MacLean blustered. "I never threatened her! I just told her what was what, and the snooty cow didn't want to hear it."

"I assume you're referring to the fact that Riley is Mr Slater's son," McCord said. "Why did you not claim child maintenance from Mr Slater straightaway?"

MacLean shifted uncomfortably in her seat. "Well, I had a boyfriend at the time. I mean, he wasn't my boyfriend when I slept with Dan, we were on a break."

She stared at McCord as if challenging him to question her innocence in this matter.

"And when you found out you were pregnant?" McCord prompted her.

"I assumed the baby was my boyfriend's. We got back together straight after."

"And when did you find out that your child was Mr Slater's?" McCord asked.

"About three months ago. Riley was sick and they did a blood test. The doctor told us Riley was type O. My boyfriend went all funny and asked the doctor if he was sure because he is type AB, and that would mean that he couldn't be Riley's dad. He works as a lab assistant, so he knows about these things. I almost fell over with the shock. He went absolutely mental, got himself a DNA test and had the birth certificate changed. He's left me and Riley without a penny. Can you imagine?"

McCord could, but he thought of what Calderwood would have said.

"That must have been a difficult situation for you."

"You bet it was. An absolute nightmare," MacLean said. "I'll never hear the end of it from my mum. She keeps going on about it, but at least she took us in while I went looking for Dan. I couldn't track him down at first, but then he was all over the papers with his lottery win, so I go to his place, but he isn't there, and the woman he's living with throws me and Riley out as if we're a piece of garbage. But Riley is Dan's son, and Riley will get what he's due."

McCord tried to think of a way to put the next question delicately but failed.

"Do you have proof that Riley is Mr Slater's son?"

MacLean was most indignant. "I don't need proof, I know. Do you think I'm a slapper?"

"It doesn't matter what I think," McCord said, "but you will have to prove that Mr Slater is the father of your child if you want to claim child support."

"No need. They'll infer, so I'll get my, eh, Riley's money at some point."

Unfamiliar with family law, McCord was not sure what she meant, but she did not stop to explain further.

"But it'll take ages! Can you not get Dan to take the test?" she asked hopefully. "He'll listen to the police. Just tell him, if he doesn't, I'll set all the papers onto him and make his life a bloody misery."

"When Mr Slater is fit to be interviewed, I'll certainly ask him about the matter," McCord said. "But in the meantime, I'd like to know where you were last Thursday around lunchtime?"

MacLean leaned forward. "You're not saying I ran Dan off the road? What would I do that for? I'm sitting here with no money coming in, remember?"

"Yes, but if Mr Slater had died in the accident, and Riley is indeed his son, he would be entitled to inherit. Has this thought never occurred to you?"

For a split second, MacLean's eyes flitted to the floor to her left, then she looked McCord straight in the eye.

"No, never," she said.

"Fine," McCord said, scribbling his notes. "But please answer my question. Where were you last Thursday between twelve and one o'clock?"

"At home with my son," MacLean spat. "Where else should I be? I can't afford childcare, can I, without having a job!"

"Can your mother confirm your alibi?" he asked impassively.

MacLean screwed up her face in an effort to remember. "She was out with a friend."

"Did she take her car?"

For the first time, he saw fear in MacLean's eyes. "No, I don't think so."

"I'll get an officer to take you downstairs to give an official statement. And please, remember that lying to the police is a punishable offence," McCord added. "Goodbye, Ms MacLean. No doubt, we will speak again."

He had barely had time to update his file when he got a text from Sutton.

"You wanted to tell me something?" he asked after being admitted to her fortress.

"Dunbar accessed Slater's accounts from her device," Sutton said.

"What? How?" For the life of him, he could not picture Dunbar as a hacker.

"Guessed or found the password?" Sutton suggested.

"So, she knew about the payments," McCord thought aloud. "Would she have seen that they went to Sarah Cartwright?"

"Yes. Purpose given was 'business'."

Sutton shifted restlessly on her chair. McCord guessed that this conversation was not over yet.

"Anything else?"

"The appraisal. Tomorrow." Her croaky voice was full of despair.

McCord really had no time to prep Sutton for the meeting with Hepburn. But he had promised. "I'll pop in later with the appraisal forms," he said.

"Here," she croaked.

She handed him the papers. Of course, there was nothing in the station's network she could not access in less than a minute.

McCord spent half an hour going over the appraisal questions with her. By the end of the session, she had spoken more than in all their conversations of the past year put together; she even managed to look McCord in the eye as she intoned that she was happy with the continuous professional development on offer and that she had no ambitions of promotion.

McCord's genuine praise consisted in a smile, and a nod that was returned. He wound his way out of the den back into the open-plan office and told the others of Sutton's discovery. Suddenly, Yvonne Dunbar had popped up as the main suspect for both cases. Maybe love, or what some considered to be love, was a stronger motive than money after all. However, proving it beyond reasonable doubt was another matter.

He walked back towards his office and handed Calderwood a twenty-pound note. "Get us a coffee and a muffin from across the road. I need some caffeine and sugar. And make sure Hepburn doesn't catch you at it."

Chapter 21

Early the next morning, Dharwan turned up at the station to update McCord on the situation at the hospital, but there was nothing more to report, apart from the ongoing tension between Slater and Dunbar. McAllister had not turned up again, and to Turner's bitter disappointment, Ross Cartwright had not made another attempt to knock off Daniel Slater.

Dharwan glanced at her phone. "I'd better go there and start my shift. Turner will be desperate to go home and get some sleep."

"I'll give you a lift," McCord said. "Calderwood and I are going to pay Slater a visit. I want him to take this paternity test, and I also want a word with the future Mrs Slater about her nosing about in his bank accounts."

Dharwan raised her eyebrows. "Did she?"

"She did."

The phone rang. As McCord listened, a big grin spread across his face. "Thank you, Turner," he said. "We'll be over asap."

He put the receiver down. Dharwan was looking at him expectantly.

"Slater's memory has come back. He wants to make a statement. Ah, perfect timing. Calderwood, come on, we're off to the Royal Infirmary. And look who's coming with us."

Calderwood beamed. His eyes locked into Dharwan's, and he seemed to forget everything around him.

"Hello, Earth calling," McCord said. "Did you get the paternity test kit? I think once Slater understands that his only way out of this is a negative test result, he'll be as keen as me to get it done as quickly as possible."

"Yes, yes, here it is."

He leaned over past Dharwan to pick up the packet from the top of the filing cabinet but stumbled and would have fallen if Dharwan had not caught him. Twisted in an awkward embrace, they started laughing, and McCord with them, when Struthers suddenly appeared in the open doorway.

"What do you want, Struthers?" McCord barked.

He was well aware of how it looked. Struthers put on a shocked expression, but McCord had seen the flicker of a smirk flit across his face.

"Apologies! Of course, I would have knocked if I had known…" he said suggestively, "I'll come back later…" Then he withdrew.

"Damn," Calderwood said. "I'm so sorry, Surina."

"It wasn't your fault," she said. "Don't worry."

But her laughter had died.

"That obnoxious toad," McCord muttered. "I bet he saw you coming in and hung around outside for an opportunity to catch you out."

They walked downstairs to the car in silence and headed for the Infirmary.

* * *

Meanwhile, Amy was sitting at Daniel Slater's bedside, watched over closely by Yvonne Dunbar.

"It's so nice to meet you at last," Amy said, beaming. "I'm glad that Yvonne persuaded you to speak to me. I can hardly write a glowing article about a man I've never met. How are you feeling?"

Slater smiled weakly. "I'm feeling great. I can't wait to get out of here."

"Don't be silly, Dan," Dunbar said. "Just because they're moving you out of the ICU, it doesn't mean that you are back to normal yet."

Slater shot her a resentful glance, and Amy wondered if he was so keen to be discharged just to get away from Dunbar.

"By the way," Amy said, "I met your brother Richard for a drink on Saturday. He is worried about you."

"Ricky?" Slater asked with a frown. "What did you meet him for?"

Amy was taken aback by the accusation in his tone. "He wants to make sure that the police are fully investigating the accident and that they will catch whoever... forced you off the road," she said, careful to avoid the word 'kill'.

"I don't know why he's getting involved," Slater said, annoyed. "We haven't spoken since..."

"Since the adoption?" Amy prompted. "I think he feels bad about that and would like to make amends."

"I don't believe that for a minute," Slater said.

He looked Amy in the eye. "It's probably an excuse to hit on you, or maybe he thinks it makes him look good, playing the concerned brother."

"Are you sure you can't give him a second chance? It seems such a shame—"

"Quite sure," Slater interrupted her. "And what business is it of yours, anyway?"

"It's entirely up to you, of course," Amy said hastily and rose. "I'll show you and Yvonne the final draft of my article before we publish it, but it won't be until next Saturday at the earliest."

Amy looked across to Dunbar, willing her to leave them alone for at least a minute, but there was no sign of that happening.

"Well," said Amy, "I'd better go and leave you to rest."

Slater smiled, and Amy thought she detected a note of regret.

"It was sweet of you to try to reconcile me with my brother," Slater said, "but some things can't be undone."

Amy smiled back.

"But forgiven, perhaps?" she asked.

She stared pointedly at Dunbar whose mouth was a thin line.

Slater shook his head.

"I really want to know who did this to you," Amy said. "Are you sure you remember nothing more about the crash?"

"I do, actually," Slater said, bright-eyed. "This morning, it all came back to me. I told PC Turner, and DI McCord himself is coming over to speak to me. If you promise not to mention my brother again, I'll tell you, too."

* * *

Always two steps ahead of Calderwood and Dharwan, McCord hurried along the corridors of the Royal Infirmary, drawing stares from patients and staff that he duly ignored. Calderwood nodded encouragingly to everybody they passed, signalling that there was no need to be alarmed.

"Come on," McCord said to Calderwood. "Stop flirting with everybody. I want this blasted accident off my books."

As they turned the last corner, McCord's pulse, already fast from running up to the first floor and along the corridor, began to race. He came to an abrupt halt, almost causing Calderwood to bump into him. In an attempt to look casual, he sauntered towards Slater's room.

"Miss Thornton," he said with an ironic smile, trying to control his breathing, "you're here very early. Please, tell me you didn't trick the hospital staff into giving you a relatives' room. Though it would make sense, of course, since you are spending such a lot of time–"

"I'm just faster off the mark than Edinburgh CID," Amy said, scrutinising his face. "And I got here without attempting to break the two-hundred-metres record. Good morning, Duncan; hello, Surina."

McCord felt himself blush, which made matters worse because his face was already glowing from exertion.

"Dan has news for you," she said. "You must be pleased that at least one of your cases has been solved without you having to figure it out."

McCord's face was the shade of morello cherries by now.

"You'll be feeling deprived now," he said. "Unless something – or somebody – else has captured your interest."

Amy looked at him quizzically. "As a matter of fact, it has. Something apart from the adoption must have happened between the two brothers. I can understand Dan being mad about being left out, even after all this time, but Richard is definitely keeping something back. There must be more to it, and I'm going to find out what that is."

"I think you're looking for a story where there is none," McCord said. "Sometimes people simply don't get on. A clash of characters that is nobody's fault."

"People who are very different can still be good together," Calderwood interjected, "but it takes two for a relationship to work."

There was a brief, uncomfortable silence that neither McCord nor Amy filled.

"Well, I think this is a very nice idea, Amy," Calderwood said, eventually. "You'd be doing a good deed reconciling the two brothers."

He looked at McCord as if inviting him to agree, but McCord was in no mood for niceties.

"You can stay here, Calderwood, if you want to have a heart-to-heart with Amy, but I'll be going in now to see what Slater has to say," McCord said. "And then I'm going back to the station to solve two murder cases."

Amy waved them goodbye. "Good luck," she said to Calderwood and Dharwan, leaving it open to interpretation whether she was referring to the murder cases or to working with McCord.

When she was out of sight, McCord turned to Calderwood. "See?" he said. "There I am being nice, and we end up having a fight."

Calderwood shook his head and sighed, but McCord had already moved on.

Outside Slater's room, Turner was pacing up and down the corridor. He stopped when he saw McCord rushing towards him.

"Has he said anything to you, Turner?"

"No, sir. He wants to talk to you personally. If he remembers who it was, he won't need protection anymore, will he?" Turner asked hopefully.

"Let's not count our chickens."

Seeing Yvonne Dunbar tripping towards them, McCord fell silent.

"Have you come to speak to Dan about the accident?" Dunbar demanded.

"We're about to," McCord said, "and we'll have this conversation in private." McCord stopped a nurse who was walking past. "Is there somewhere Ms Dunbar can wait until we have finished talking to Mr Slater?"

"There is a family room down the corridor, on the right," the nurse said and hurried on.

"PC Dharwan, would you keep Ms Dunbar company while she's waiting?"

If it had been Dunbar who had tried to kill Slater, he was not going to give her the opportunity to give them the slip; Dharwan did not need him to spell it out. "Of course," she said. "Do come along, Ms Dunbar."

With Turner lingering at the door, McCord and Calderwood approached Slater, who was sitting up with an expectant smile.

"Thank you for coming so quickly," he said to McCord. "At long last I've got my memory back, and I can't wait to tell you."

"Do you remember the accident now?" McCord asked, sitting down at the bedside.

"Yes, as clear as day. I was driving home from the station" – he lowered his head – "a bit too fast, I'm afraid. You see, I was quite upset after meeting Sarah's husband, and as I was driving along, a car came up behind me, far too close. I checked the mirror, and recognised Ross Cartwright's car. Sarah had used it once when we met. I sped up to get away from him but didn't want to go too much over the speed limit. On that long, straight stretch of the road, he suddenly pulled out and drove alongside me. I saw his face and I knew he wanted me dead."

He rubbed his face with his hands as if to get rid of the memory he had only just retrieved from his subconscious. "He then came closer and closer; I lost my nerve and swerved off the road. And the rest you know."

McCord was up from his seat before Slater had finished the sentence.

"Thank you very much, Mr Slater," he said. "At least now we know. We'll prepare a statement for you to sign later."

Calderwood closed his notebook and rose as well.

"Is that going to help you to get Cartwright for Sarah's murder?" Slater asked. "Because that's what really matters to me. I'll be alright, but she…" His voice trailed off as he buried his face in his hands.

"I can't make any promises," McCord said. "But we'll do everything we can."

Slater looked up. "Thank you," he said.

McCord was about to say goodbye when Calderwood caught his eye, waving the test kit about and looking questioningly at him. McCord was keen to get back to the station, but he thought that Slater could do with a bit of advice.

"Since Ms MacLean is innocent, we have no further interest in your private affairs, Mr Slater," he said, "but she told us she is pursuing the paternity dispute through the courts and is thinking of going to the press. Nobody can force you to do the test, but having it done is the only way. If it's negative, the whole story goes away. If you are the father, you should come to an arrangement with Ms MacLean as soon as possible. It's not only the right thing to do, it also saves you from a much greater mess."

Slater sighed. "I know you mean well, DI McCord. I'll do that. Thank you."

McCord joined Turner at the doorway.

"It was Cartwright after all. Call the station and put out a warrant for Cartwright's arrest."

"Are you not going back yet?" Turner asked.

"Still got a few loose ends to tie up," McCord said. "Tell them, I'll be back soon. And you'd better get some sleep."

* * *

Calderwood followed McCord into the family room where Yvonne Dunbar and Dharwan were silently sitting opposite each other on broad, upholstered chairs. McCord was unfazed by Dunbar's open hostility towards him.

"PC Dharwan, please take over from PC Turner," McCord said.

Dharwan rose swiftly. "Of course, sir." With a furtive smile at Calderwood, she left.

The family room was a calm and comfortable space with upholstered chairs, a coffee table and prints of floral paintings hanging on the walls. McCord suspected that it was here that relatives were given a cup of tea to help them cope with any bad news, so in a way, it was very appropriate for this meeting. Parched from his earlier physical and emotional exertions, McCord helped himself to a cup from the water dispenser in the corner.

As the cold, clear liquid rose, McCord watched Dunbar pull down her tight dress, only for it to ride up again when she lowered herself gingerly onto the seat. In an effort to look relaxed, she leant back, but the seat was too long for her thighs, and she ended up slumped halfway down the chair. She pulled herself up again and crossed her legs. Having regained control over her position, she turned to McCord with a haughty expression.

"Well, at least we all know now what happened to my Dan. Not that you lot have been much use. But I don't want an apology, I just want to get back to my boyfriend."

A mirthless smile made McCord's mouth twitch.

"Not just yet. We know that you accessed Mr Slater's accounts. You must have wondered why he was transferring money to another woman. My guess is that you suspected then that he was having an affair with Sarah Cartwright. And I wonder, of course, why you lied about this during your interview."

Dunbar sat stock-still for a moment; then she recovered her composure. "I did have my suspicions, but Dan swore there was nothing between him and Sarah Cartwright, that he was simply investing in her new business. I believed him, and when she died–"

"Your problem was solved," McCord finished the sentence. "But why were you checking his accounts in the first place if you weren't jealous?"

"I wanted to know what was happening to our… the money," Dunbar said. "At first, it was, yeah, you can have what you want, babe, and next thing all I heard was, no, we don't need that, and we need to be careful what we spend and blah-blah-blah. I'm not stupid, I know that there would be over two hundred thousand pounds in interest each year, even after we'd bought the house, the cars and the rest. I asked Dan straight out what was going on, but he was cagey and said something about the current economic climate, looking after our pensions and other bullshit. So, I got into his computer."

She looked at McCord as if that settled the matter.

"Did you know Mr Slater's password and banking details?" Calderwood asked, taking notes.

"He can't remember things, so he writes everything down. I searched his phone when he was in the shower, and there it all was, in his notes."

Dunbar seemed pleased with her investigative prowess.

"I find it hard to believe that you took the discovery of a potential rival lying down," McCord said. "Did you not try to find out exactly what was happening?"

Dunbar shrugged.

"I was going to, but Dan was suddenly amazing again, like when we first met. He even agreed to buying me a horse, something he had refused me so many times before, so I thought, if he made a mistake, he's learned his lesson; it's best to let sleeping dogs lie. Everything was fine, and then, bang, he comes off the road. Then it turns out it was this guy, Cartwright. Are you going to arrest him or not?"

"We are going to arrest him for the attempted murder of your boyfriend, don't you worry. The problem is, Ms Dunbar," McCord said, "we have no conclusive evidence that Mr Cartwright killed his wife. On the other hand, we have you with a very strong motive, means and opportunity, but without an alibi."

Dunbar paled under her make-up. "I told you I was shopping!"

"Nobody remembers seeing you, and my colleagues have spent hours going through CCTV without spotting you anywhere you said you were. It is also very uncharacteristic of you to make only a small cash purchase and not keeping the receipt. Looking at your credit card transactions, you rarely go out without spending a lot more than ten pounds on a box of chocolates."

Dunbar's expression hardened. Whether she was appalled at hearing that nobody remembered her or she understood the trouble she was in, McCord was not sure.

"Well, I did that time," she said. "You'll just have to believe me."

"The problem is that lying seems to come easy to you, Ms Dunbar," he said, rising from his chair, making to leave. "But remember: judges don't like people who lie to the police, and sooner or later, we will find out the truth."

"Knock yourself out," Dunbar said, and without looking at the detectives, she took a sizeable pouch out of her bag and began to reapply her make-up.

* * *

"What do you think?" McCord asked Calderwood as soon as they were outside. "She could easily have made it to the Crags and back in time."

Calderwood was sceptical. "In one of her outfits?"

"She had time to change. Slater was busy with putting up the billiard table, so he wouldn't have noticed the state she was in when she came back. Pity, if we'd known at the time, we could have checked her wardrobe. It'll all be washed or got rid of by now if that's what happened."

"How would she have known when Sarah Cartwright went jogging?" Calderwood asked.

"Sarah Cartwright had a strict routine, her husband said. Dunbar has nothing to do all day. She could easily have followed Sarah Cartwright and found out what she did in the evenings."

"You're not convinced it was the husband anymore?" Calderwood asked.

"For the moment," McCord said, "I'll keep an open mind."

Chapter 22

The next day, Amy spent hunched over her computer putting together her feature on lottery winners. It had been greatly spiced up by Daniel Slater's revelation that the jealous husband of his lover had tried to kill him, and Amy was hoping to get the article out before the other papers cottoned on. And yet, she could not shake off the feeling that she was missing an essential part of the story, and that Richard McAllister was at the centre of it.

Why had he been adopted, and his brother hadn't? What was Richard McAllister holding back? She would have to speak to somebody who knew the boys at the time.

She had just found the contact details of Richard McAllister's adoptive parents when her phone rang. It was Douglas, the pastry chef. With a sudden pang of guilt, Amy realised that she hadn't called him back about a proposed night out at Lane7 with his friends. She sighed. A while ago, an evening of bowling and cocktails with an admirer had been exactly what she was after, and Douglas always did his best to entertain her.

Ever since their first date, her evenings had been filled with visits to pubs, restaurants and the cinema, with or without Douglas's friends. No more lonely gin and tonics for her! He obviously wanted to take the relationship to the next level, and she couldn't think of any reason to refuse him. He ticked every one of her boxes – he was attentive, cheerful and obviously smitten – but still the expected bliss had failed to materialise. Rather than included, she was beginning to feel crowded by his friends, and the relentless entertainment left her inexplicably bored.

Her new social life had plunged Martin into a state of permanent anxiety, but her pride had not yet allowed her to admit even to herself that the pastry chef failed to fire her up. She declined the call and composed a message. 'Sorry, can't make it tonight, something's come up at work'. After a moment's deliberation, she placed a small 'x' after it. If she didn't, Douglas would ask what was wrong, and she was not ready to have this conversation just yet.

Instead, she dialled the home number of Richard McAllister's adoptive parents.

* * *

The following morning, Amy was climbing the stairs to the flat on the top floor of a stone-built tenement in Spottiswoode Road to have morning coffee with George and Karen McAllister.

She was thinking about the two estranged brothers, already picturing herself as the person who would unearth a long-buried family secret and bring about the long overdue reconciliation between them. Everybody would be grateful to her and her article would have that feel-good factor that was sometimes missing in the tragic and violent cases she covered.

Amy had expected a far grander dwelling for somebody working in oil and gas. The smiling lady who opened the door wore slacks and a light cotton jumper, which Amy immediately identified as being off the shelf. She wondered for a moment if the woman was the housekeeper.

"Hello, I'm Karen McAllister. Do come in, Miss Thornton."

"Amy, please. Thank you so much for seeing me," Amy said as she stepped into the hall.

"It's a pleasure," Karen McAllister said. "Both my husband and I are great fans of *Forth Write* magazine.

153

Every Saturday at breakfast time, we fight over it. George reads the articles by your colleague Martin Eden, and I read yours. We often end up cutting the magazine up."

She laughed as she showed Amy into a large sitting room with a bay window looking out over the rooftops. On the coffee table, she had laid out a plate with home-made scones, generously filled with jam and cream, and a little bowl with chocolates.

"Please, have a seat. Tea? Coffee?"

"Coffee, please."

"Milk? Sugar?"

"Just milk, thanks."

Amy waited until Karen McAllister had disappeared into the kitchen to have a good look round. On one of the walls hung the painted portrait of a boy, about twelve. It wasn't a very good likeness of Richard, Amy thought. The blond, wavy hair shone like his, but the eyes and mouth were all wrong. There was a piano in the corner with a dozen family photographs on it, but Amy was too far away to see who was in them. Through the open door she could see an absurdly long corridor, and it was then she realised that two flats had been knocked together to form a very spacious home.

"I'm afraid George had to see to an urgent matter at work," Karen McAllister said as she brought in two large mugs of coffee topped with foamed milk and put them down on the table. "He was very sorry to miss you. We were wondering last night why you would come to see us. We lead a very boring life, really, and I can assure you, we have nothing to do with any crime – or fashion." She laughed again. "Please help yourself to a scone."

"I'm writing an article on lottery winners," Amy said, "and I've been chatting to Daniel Slater."

She bit into her scone. It was light and a little crumbly, and the jam tasted home-made, too.

"Ah," Karen McAllister said, still smiling. "You found out that he is our Richard's half-brother. Still, I don't quite see how we can help. We're not in contact with Daniel at all."

"That's exactly why I wanted to speak to you. Richard told me about the adoption, and I had a sense that he is sad that Daniel won't have anything to do with him."

Karen McAllister nodded. "Yes, he was very upset when he heard about the car accident. He went to the hospital as soon as he heard, but Daniel wouldn't see him."

"It's such a shame," Amy said. "I seem to be the only one who is in contact with both of them, so maybe I can help, but I need to understand what happened when they were boys."

Karen McAllister suddenly seemed anxious. "You must think that we are horrible people."

Surprised, Amy put down her mug. "Why would I think that?"

"Because we didn't adopt Daniel as well."

"I did wonder about it," Amy admitted, "but I'm sure you had a good reason."

Karen McAllister cradled her mug.

"It was a difficult time for all of us. George and I often wondered how Daniel was doing. To be honest, we were quite relieved when he won the lottery. He deserved a lucky break, and it made us feel a little less guilty about not adopting him."

"So why didn't you?" Amy asked.

Karen McAllister pointed to the portrait on the wall.

"When our Sammy died, our world came to an end. I couldn't have any more children, so a friend suggested we adopt."

She fell silent, fighting back tears.

Amy tried not to show her surprise. She had thought the painting was the work of an incompetent painter, but now it turned out that the lost son was almost Richard's doppelganger.

"I'm so sorry." Amy's heartfelt pity, however, was tinged with disapproval. Poor Richard. A replacement for a dead child.

"I know what you're thinking," Karen McAllister said, having composed herself. "But it wasn't like that."

There was an urgency in her voice that encouraged Amy to probe deeper.

"What was it like?"

"George and I both wanted a child again, wanted to be parents again. Richard was about the same age as Sammy, and he did look a lot like him, that is true, but he was so troubled. Traumatised. He needed parents just as we needed a child. Social services were very keen for the brothers to stay together, so we considered having them both. That day, the next-door flat came on the market. It seemed like a sign, so we bought it and knocked the walls through to create more space for our new family."

"Why didn't you just move into a bigger place?" Amy asked, but as soon as she had asked the question, she bit her tongue.

Karen McAllister looked across to the painting. "I feel close to Sammy here. So many memories. It is as if I haven't lost him altogether. Silly, I know."

"Not at all," Amy said.

She couldn't begin to imagine what it must be like to lose a child. It was frightening to think how vulnerable one was as a parent. Every day, the possibility of being utterly devastated lurked just around the corner.

Karen McAllister was still gazing at her first son, lost in memories.

Amy waited in silence until she came out of her reverie. Gently, Amy brought her back to the original question.

"I'm sure you've been a wonderful mother to both your sons. Can you tell me why it didn't work out with Daniel?"

Karen McAllister hesitated. "Please, don't write this in your article. Richard would be mortified, and George would be angry with me for saying this."

Amy was intrigued but nodded. "We won't print anything about your private affairs without your permission."

Karen McAllister sighed. "Richard didn't want Daniel to live with us. When we asked why, he said they didn't get on, and he wanted it to be just us. George and I were quite shocked, and God forgive us, we even considered not taking Richard; it seemed such a selfish, brutal thing to say. But then we thought, these children had been so deprived of love, without a father, and the mother an alcoholic. And poor Richard found her as well."

"Found her?" Amy asked.

"Yes, she'd had a stroke. She was lying on the sofa, unconscious, when he came home after playing football outside. Daniel was in the kitchen making dinner. He'd always looked after Richard because their mother was neglecting them terribly. Imagine! I still wonder why she didn't get help before it came to that. I understand that some people destroy themselves, but if you have children... wouldn't a mother do anything to protect them? Anything?"

Amy nodded but thought that Karen McAllister was rather naïve, both where addiction and mothering instincts were concerned.

"We had long conversations with the boys' social worker – Graham Knight, he was called. Such a nice young man," Karen McAllister went on. "The preference is always for siblings to stay together, and he tried to get us to take in both boys because Daniel's chances of being adopted were pretty much zero. Everybody wants babies, apparently, so children over the age of six are rarely put up for adoption, and the boys were twelve and fourteen at that point. But Richard blankly refused to be with Daniel."

"And he never said why?"

Karen McAllister shook her head.

"To be fair to Richard, when we first met the boys together, I felt there was... hatred is too strong a word, more like resentment in Daniel towards Richard. I couldn't put my finger on it, and Graham Knight, the social worker, didn't have an explanation either. But Daniel didn't say anything explicitly, and it was obvious that he wanted to stay with us. He was so sweet and polite, and I wondered if I had just imagined the whole thing. My husband George and I discussed it at length; we decided it would be right to keep the brothers together. We were sure whatever issues they had could be resolved, but Richard wouldn't hear of it. He was screaming and shouting, even saying he didn't want to be adopted if it wasn't him alone, so in the end, the social worker felt that it would be no good to force the issue."

"So, you fostered and then adopted Richard on his own," Amy said.

"Yes. Daniel was such a lovely boy, quiet and well-behaved. Cute, too with his freckles and blue eyes. But Richard was the younger and much needier of the two and, to be honest, I had my heart set on him at first sight, so we chose him, and Daniel went to other foster parents. Graham Knight assured us he would be well looked after."

"And you never found out why Richard and Daniel didn't get on?" Amy asked. "You'd think that such a background would bring them closer together."

Karen McAllister shrugged. "To be honest, we had too many other issues with Richard to worry about Daniel. We had the police round a few times because he had been shoplifting and vandalising the school. After a while, he calmed down, though, and has been nothing but a joy since. It was probably just a clash of characters with Richard being so wild then."

"I think it would be wonderful if the two made up. A sibling is, after all, family, and for them, the only relative they've got."

Seeing the hurt in Karen McAllister's eyes, she quickly added, "In terms of blood relations, I mean."

"We did try," Karen McAllister said. "But for the first year or so, Richard flatly refused to have anything to do with Daniel. Once he had settled down and had had counselling, things got better, and he was desperate to make up with his brother. I was so happy for both of them, but Daniel ignored Richard's cards and presents, and when Richard visited him on his eighteenth birthday, Daniel was very rude to him and told him to leave him alone. It has been so upsetting for Richard. I have no idea what is going on in that boy's head. Daniel's, I mean." She smiled. "At least, now, he has no money worries anymore; compared to him, we are paupers. Hopefully, that will make him feel better."

"He's not feeling great at the moment," Amy said. "So far, the money has brought him nothing but trouble, which is going to be the whole point of my article."

"What a shame. The poor boy. Do tell him we all wish him the very best, Richard in particular, of course."

Amy rose. "Thank you so much for your time and the scone; it was delicious."

"I'm sorry that I couldn't help you with your article," Karen McAllister said. "It would have been such fun to be mentioned in our favourite magazine."

Amy slowly descended the stairs to the ground floor. She was no closer to figuring out what had happened between Richard and Dan, but she did have a name. Graham Knight.

* * *

Back at the magazine offices, Martin seemed relieved to be distracted from the latest squabbles in the Scottish parliament and more than willing to hear Amy's thoughts on the tale of the two brothers. Today, Martin had gone for the tortured rock singer look. Clad, uncharacteristically, entirely in black leather, with eyes surrounded by dark eyeliner and blood-red lips, he reminded Amy of a vampire at a funeral.

"Who's died?" Amy asked with a grin. "Your hope of Scottish independence?"

"Never," Martin said. "It's just that the general state of the world is utterly depressing." He folded one long, thin leg over the other. "Now, cheer me up and tell me about two brothers who are both wealthy beyond my imagination and yet desperately unhappy."

He listened to Amy's account of her meeting with the family without interrupting.

"The story doesn't add up," Amy summarised. "Why were the boys so at odds with each other even before the adoption? Richard must have done something terrible to Dan before the McAllisters came on the scene, something he was even sent to a therapist for. The mother said he was a real handful, but what a horrible thing to do to ruin his brother's adoption. Why would he do that? He seems such a nice guy, and he told me he tried so hard for so long to make amends."

"Maybe you are being taken in by Richard's charms. Maybe he was a nasty piece of work and still is. The McAllisters don't see it that way, of course, and probably pressured Richard into making up with Dan, but he didn't really try because he got all he wanted. He got the wealthy parents to himself, and no doubt a sizeable inheritance down the line. But now that Dan is a millionaire, he has become much more attractive as a brother."

"I suppose, Richard could be after the money," Amy said. "Dan even warned me off and suggested that Richard only arranged our meeting because he fancies me."

"That seems highly likely," Martin said, "since you are utterly adorable."

"Nonsense," Amy said, her ponytail swinging to and fro as she shook her head. "He was very pleasant—"

"Aren't they all, when they want something? You can be a little bit naïve, darling, where the male species is concerned. You have no idea what you can do to a man's heart. Speaking of which, how are things with doughy Douglas?"

"He is very sweet," she countered.

"Too much sugar is bad for you."

"When you're done with your innuendo, can we get back to Richard?" she said irritably. "The mother–"

"You can't take everything the mother says at face value," Martin said. "Whatever slant she puts on it, adopting a boy who is so like her own dead son is unhealthy. Maybe she is projecting her own rejection of Dan onto Richard."

"She was quite open about it, though," Amy said. "And apart from the grief over her son, she seemed a happy, well-balanced person. Something about the whole thing is bugging me."

Martin shook his head.

"Whatever is going on in that family, it doesn't look as if you'll achieve a reconciliation after all this time, so why don't you let it go and concentrate on the other lottery winners or, even better, help DI McCord solve the Cartwright case?"

"I'm not sure what I can do. They've checked out both Sarah Cartwright's husband and Yvonne Dunbar, but they don't seem to be able to prove either of them did it. I phoned Duncan earlier and he told me they're about to release Ross Cartwright without charge. Even Dan's witness statement isn't enough to hold him without corroborating evidence or a confession."

"What about the other woman, the one with the child? Have they got proof that Daniel is the father yet?"

"Apparently, he agreed to do a test. The results will go to him and Kimberley, but I don't know when. They might not be overly keen to tell us either."

"Have you spoken to this Amanda Jackson again?" Martin asked with a little smile.

Amy pulled a face. "After that fiasco with her boyfriend? Not likely. I got that spectacularly wrong."

Martin patted her hand. "Never mind, my darling. At least DI McCord was there in a flash. I keep telling you he's yours for the taking. What is he planning to do next?"

"I don't know," Amy said.

"Well, why don't you go to St Leonard's to find out?"

Amy bristled.

"You know very well why not. There's no way I'm giving the impression of running after him."

Martin gave a theatrical sigh.

Amy's eyes narrowed.

"And don't you dare go to the station and play Cupid, understood?" she said.

Every inch of him pretending wronged innocence, Martin heaved an even deeper sigh and returned to his reflections on the state of the nation. Amy swivelled back and forth on her chair, contemplating her next move. Martin was right, of course. There was nothing she would have loved more than to go to St Leonard's, but she felt she could not turn up empty-handed.

She checked her social media feeds in the vain hope of another murder in the city, but her thoughts kept returning to the two brothers. Even if there was no crime involved, she knew she would not have any peace of mind until she found out what had happened between them before the McAllisters appeared on the scene and brought it all to a head with their adoption plans. She called up the file on Daniel Slater she had compiled for her first interview with Yvonne Dunbar and added the name of his former social worker, Graham Knight.

All she needed to find out was where he was working now, and tomorrow, she would pay him a visit.

Chapter 23

The following morning, Amy was heading towards the north-west of the city. After a little detective work, she had found out that Graham Knight now worked at the Barnardo's Caern Project on Gogarmuir Road, a place providing respite care for children with learning disabilities.

Leaving the heavy traffic on the bypass behind, she found herself driving along a pleasant country lane and parked at what looked to be an old, stone-built farmhouse complex.

Inside, she was met by the receptionist who had a receiver clamped between her ear and shoulder and was taking notes while rummaging through some files on her desk. She smiled apologetically at Amy and motioned her to wait.

"Yes," the receptionist said to the caller, "of course, I will. Bye for now." She put the receiver down. "Can I help you?"

"I'd like to speak to–"

The phone rang again.

"Sorry!"

Amy listened to a lengthy conversation about arranging care for a severely autistic child and wished she had phoned. But then again, what she wanted from Graham Knight was somewhat irregular. In her job, she had found that face-to-face conversations always yielded better results, especially if the other party had no time to prepare answers beforehand.

At long last, the child had been booked in, and the receptionist turned to Amy.

"I was wondering if I could have a quick word with Graham," Amy said. "I know he is busy, but I won't keep him more than a minute, I promise."

The receptionist picked up the receiver. "What name shall I say?"

Amy's heart began to beat faster. "Amy. He doesn't know me but a friend of mine needs his help. Urgently," she added to pre-empt further questions.

The receptionist looked intrigued and made the call.

A couple of minutes later, a very tall, broad man in jeans and a jumper displaying the Guinness Beer toucan emerged from inside the building and walked towards her. His shrewd eyes locked into hers, and while his smile was warm and encouraging, she suspected that he had taken in more about her than she might have liked.

"Your name is Amy? I'm Graham. How can I help?"

His voice bubbled as if he was ready to laugh any second. Amy could see why Richard and Karen McAllister had liked him. She'd only been in his company for a few seconds and was already wondering if he was single, but the view of his ring finger was obstructed by a blue latex glove. A quick calculation supported by the crinkles around his eyes put him somewhere in his late thirties, but his bouncing gait made him seem younger.

"Are you in trouble?" he asked, serious now.

Amy realised that she had not answered his first question. She suspected he got that a lot.

"Would you mind if we went outside?" she asked with a glance at the receptionist.

Knight hesitated, but then pointed to the door and followed her outside into the courtyard. Next to a tall fuchsia whose bright-red flowers swayed in the cool breeze, Amy slowed and turned to Knight, who quickly lifted his gaze to her eyes. Was he really blushing, or was she imagining it? Stop it, she told herself. You're not here to flirt.

"I'm a friend of Daniel Slater and his brother Ricky," she said, making it sound as if they were best buddies. "Do you remember them? Ricky told me you used to be their social worker about ten, twelve years ago."

"Of course, I remember them," Knight said. He sounded cheery, but Amy noticed that there was something guarded in his manner now. "The boys were some of my first clients when I started working in social services. How is Dan? I read about the car crash; is he alright?"

Amy thought it very endearing that he mentioned the accident rather than the lottery win.

"He's out of immediate danger," she said. This was not a lie, and it furthered her cause. "But he and Ricky are still not on speaking terms, and it's having a serious impact on their mental health and on Dan's recovery."

"I'm sorry to hear that." There was sadness in his voice but Amy detected no surprise.

A sudden gust of air blew a strand of hair across her mouth. She tucked it behind her ear.

Knight followed her every movement.

"Ricky told me that this rift is going back to the time their mother died. As their social worker, you knew them then, so I was wondering—"

The mention of his former job seemed to remind Knight of his professional duties.

"You understand that I can't divulge personal information on former clients," Knight said, stiffly. Then his voice softened again. "If you want to help them, encourage them to get a mediator or even counselling. They both had a lot to deal with at that time."

Amy tried not to let her frustration show.

"Thank you," she said, slowly turning to go.

"You wouldn't like to have dinner with me, perhaps, sometime?" his rich baritone sounded at her back.

She spun round.

"I'd love that. When does your shift end?"

He seemed flustered. He clearly had not expected a yes.

"Eh… at seven. Is eight too late for you?"

"No, I'm busy until then anyway," she fibbed. "Where do you want to go?"

She could see him frantically searching his brain for the best option.

"Do you know the Italian opposite the Playhouse?" he said eventually. "I love the place. It's not easy to get a table, but once the theatregoers have left, it's usually quieter."

Amy smiled.

"Sounds great. I'll meet you there at eight."

With a coquettish smile she waved him goodbye. A date with a caring, cheerful hunk. And maybe, just maybe, after a few drinks, she would get him to tell her what she so much wanted to know.

* * *

Mamma Roma was a cosy, family-run restaurant where Graham Knight was greeted enthusiastically by Giovanni, the owner's son. The downstairs dining area was still busy, but they managed to get a table for two by the window.

As they were studying the menu, Knight every so often stole a glance at Amy. When they had ordered grilled fish skewers and a pizza parmigiana with a bottle of Chianti, Knight cleared his throat.

"So, what do you do?" he asked.

Amy busied herself with the napkin. "I work for a magazine. The fashion desk."

Knight smiled. "That figures."

"Why?"

"Well, you look… very stylish. Unlike me," he added. "I was going to go home to change, but something came up at work and I couldn't just leave."

"Of course not," Amy said. "You know, all these pleats, lapels and forever moving hemlines can get too much. To be honest, a sweatshirt and jeans is a bit of a relief. So, why did you switch from the council to Barnardo's?"

"There was a lot of turmoil in the sector. Some of the care homes closed because of the abuse scandals, and I always felt I couldn't do the kids justice. Some of them were very challenging, and after ten years, I needed a break, so when Barnardo's were looking for a manager, I went for it. But sometimes I miss my old job. When you get one of those poor kids who never had a chance in life, and you've got them into a good foster home or even adopted, you know you've made a real difference."

"Like with Ricky?" Amy ventured. "He's certainly turned out well. Amazing what a loving family and a private education can do."

Knight beamed. "That's great to hear. Ricky was wild back then. He could have gone either way, I suppose. What's he doing these days?"

"He's recently started in his adoptive father's company. Chemical engineering."

"Good for him," Knight said. "And Dan won the lottery, I hear. I suspect he's squirrelled it all away into several accounts somewhere safe. After the mess at home, he was craving order and security."

He paused, checking himself. Amy decided that he needed a little prompt.

"Ricky told me that Dan was looking after him all those years before the mother died and he did his best to keep him out of trouble." Easy does it, she said to herself. Don't spook him now. "That's why it's so strange that Dan blocks him out like that, especially when Ricky has tried so hard to make amends for whatever he did."

"It was complicated. And quite disturbing," Knight began, but then the food arrived.

Silently cursing poor Giovanni, Amy slid a piece of monkfish off the skewer and professed to be delighted with it. She was about to ask Knight what he had wanted to say, when a little old lady approached the table with a mixture of awe and determination. At the table behind the woman, a shrivelled man, who Amy suspected was the long-suffering husband, cringed with embarrassment and shot resentful glances at his wife.

"You are Amy Thornton, aren't you?" the woman said in a voice that reminded Amy of the witches in the Grimms' fairy tales her mother had subjected her to as a child. "When is DI McCord going to arrest Sarah Cartwright's husband? Everybody says it was him, all the papers are full of it, but they don't know the half of it, so I said to Eric here, that's Amy Thornton, the journalist, over there. She'll be able to tell me what's going on. We can't have a monster like him roaming our streets, can we?"

Normally, Amy would have been amused at the thought that Eric's wife had very good reason to fear homicidal husbands, but she noticed that Knight's easy smile had disappeared, and the brightness had left his eyes.

"I really have nothing to do with the police anymore," Amy said, desperately trying to limit the damage done by the nosey old crone.

"What?" she screeched. "There'll be no more of your articles on the murders in Edinburgh? Then you can tell your boss, I won't buy *Forth Write* magazine anymore!"

Seeing her mission failed, the old woman turned her back on Amy, having ruined the evening and quite possibly the happiness of two people in less than two minutes.

It took Amy a while before she had gathered the courage to meet Knight's eyes.

"So, you're a journalist. Working with the police," he said.

It was less a question than a statement. He sat quietly for a few, very long moments, while Amy pleaded with him.

"Graham, it's not what you think, I really want to help those guys, I'd never print–"

But Knight had pushed his chair back and stood up.

"Could I have a box to take away my pizza, please," he said to Giovanni, who had rushed over to see what was going on. "I've suddenly lost my appetite. The lady is going to settle the bill. She can claim it back on her expenses."

Mortified, Amy stared at the skin forming on the cooling mustard sauce covering the pale-looking fish. She dared not move until Knight had stormed out with his boxed-up pizza and Giovanni had returned to her table.

"Would you like the bill now, madam?" he asked, but she felt this was not a question either.

"Yes, please," she said.

Under his disapproving look, she swiped her card on the machine.

"Next time you see Graham, could you please tell him I'm sorry?" she asked, close to tears.

Giovanni's shrug expressed the same scepticism one might display if asked to solve the problems in the Middle East.

"Would you like your food packed up as well?" he asked, his voice softer now.

Amy shook her head.

"No, thanks. I'm sure it would have been great," she said, referring to both the meal and spending the evening with Knight.

* * *

She stepped outside into a blustery shower that sent her hair flying all over her face. Without thinking, she hit number three on her phone.

It took four rings until McCord answered.

"What's up?"

"You need to get your hands on Richard McAllister's social care file," Amy said.

"Are you still on about those two?" McCord asked. "I thought you'd be too busy in the evenings these days."

"What... ah. Has Martin been in touch with you by any chance?"

"He's worried about you. You should be grateful to have such a good friend."

"I'll thank him while I'm strangling him," said Amy. "He had no right. It's none of your business, either of you!"

To her disgust, she felt tears choking her.

"Of course not," McCord said hastily. "I shouldn't have mentioned it at all. I'm sorry. What was it you wanted to say about McAllister?"

Amy took a deep breath.

"Something happened between the brothers. I've just had dinner with their social worker, a Graham Knight–"

"Dinner?" McCord blurted out. "What did your new boyfriend think about that?"

"He can think what he likes. And yes, dinner," Amy said. "A bottle of Chianti with a nice meal loosens more tongues than being grilled in an interview room."

"I'll put a suggestion to that effect into my next appraisal," McCord replied. "What did this Knight guy say?"

"Not much," Amy admitted. "We were interrupted before he got to the details."

"Interrupted? How?"

"Never mind," Amy said. "Are you going to get those files or not?"

"Richard McAllister isn't a suspect in the car crash anymore. Slater has identified Cartwright as the culprit, so we need to concentrate on finding evidence that will stand up in court. And I can't see how Slater's childhood squabbles with his brother help me solve the two murders we're still dealing with."

"But–"

"Amy, I can only request confidential private information if there is a valid reason, so I'm afraid I can't."

"Can't or won't?" Amy asked. "All you need to do is ask Sutton. You're not usually so fussy about privacy laws."

"I do respect the law," McCord said. "I only… circumvent it if it helps me catch a killer. I'm not doing it just for–"

"Just for fun? That's what you think this is?"

"I didn't mean–"

"Well, you'd better go back to your serious policing then," Amy said, her voice dripping with sarcasm, "seeing the tremendous success you've had so far."

Blinded by tears of fury, it took her three attempts to stab the red icon.

Chapter 24

McCord had had a frustrating day. Desperate to get some kind of result before the weekend, he had pushed his team to follow up even the most outlandish claims in relation to the Sandhu case, but so far, the re-enactment had yielded nothing useful whatsoever. They had also been unable to link Sarah Cartwright to his murder. Apart from her affair with Slater, she did not seem to have any dark secrets. Calderwood had approached Amanda Jackson again, who had merely laughed at the idea of Sarah murdering Sandhu. But then, she had not been a very reliable witness so far. Unfortunately, they could not establish an alibi for Sarah

Cartwright either because her husband had been at work that night.

Not even with the car accident had there been any progress. Despite their renewed efforts, no independent witness had come forward, so they were stuck in a situation of claim and counterclaim that would not lead to a conviction. As a result, there was little he could offer Hepburn at their daily briefing.

Hepburn, on the other hand, had several points she wanted to discuss.

"I've done Heather's appraisal," she said, "and I'm very grateful to you for warning me about her… issues. Her autism does affect her communication skills rather badly, doesn't it? And she seemed extremely anxious despite me being as gentle as I could."

"She is a great asset to every investigation," McCord said. "I can handle her."

"I'm sure you can," Hepburn said. "Your immediate team is very complimentary about your leadership."

McCord did not show his surprise but sent a quiet 'thank you' towards heaven.

"However," Hepburn continued, "I have to consider her welfare as well as the station's. The other officers tell me that she almost exclusively interacts with you, which means she is of very limited use in a murder investigation. We need people with good team-working skills who can take on a variety of tasks. I also think she would be far more comfortable in an IT setting."

Suddenly, McCord felt sick. He had never thought there would be a real danger of Sutton being moved elsewhere, and now he realised he'd made her a promise he might not be able to keep.

"DC Sutton has been instrumental in solving every murder she has worked on with me," McCord said. "She is comfortable with me, and it would be a huge mistake to transfer her. It might well be the end of her career—"

"Yes, I read in her file that she was in big trouble before she came here," Hepburn interrupted. "Arthur took quite a risk when he took her on. She could be a real liability. Do you know that her nickname is 'Heather the Hacker'?"

McCord nodded, silently cursing whoever had mentioned this fact to Hepburn.

"And this is not the only occasion one of Arthur's decisions has been, shall we say, questionable," Hepburn continued. "Because I also heard that he seemed to have it in for you, which shows very poor judgement indeed."

"He wasn't wrong about Sutton," McCord said. "She's a real asset, and I need her in my team because of her IT skills. I want to keep her here."

Hepburn regarded him with a puzzled smile. "If I hadn't met Heather in person, I would have suspected another motive for your passionate defence."

McCord did not comment.

"Talking about passion," she continued, "it has come to my attention that two members of your team are in a relationship, which could constitute a serious breach of professional conduct, especially since the male concerned is of a higher rank, and therefore in a position to exploit the situation."

This time he would really kill Struthers. He would.

Hepburn's eyes were on him again. "You know who I'm talking about, Russell?"

McCord quickly weighed up the odds. Was she only fishing, then he would land Calderwood and Dharwan in it, or did she know, and it was better to try to save them from a disciplinary hearing? Considering Struthers' modus operandi, he decided to go for the latter.

"Knowing both Calderwood and Dharwan well, there is no reason whatsoever to worry. I am far more concerned about Struthers, who has repeatedly tried to make life difficult for both of them. I'm telling you, a recent incident he may have told you about was entirely innocent. I was there."

"Every time I speak to you, Russell, I am struck by the loyalty you show to your team, and I love that about you." She stressed the word 'love' in a way that sent a whole set of alarm bells pealing in McCord's mind. "I worry, though, that this supersedes your loyalty towards the rules and regulations we as professionals have to adhere to."

"But Struthers—"

"I think I have the measure of Walter, don't worry. You have indicated before that he is lazy and incompetent, and I'm keeping a close eye on him. Still, he only brought to my attention what I should have heard from you, Russell. If there is something going on between two officers, I'm duty-bound to take action."

"There really is no need," McCord said, desperately.

"The problem is, Russell, that you are too soft-hearted. If you give people too much freedom, they'll do what they like, rather than what they should. But don't worry, one of the reasons why I'm here is to take that burden off you."

Having been dismissed with much praise and encouragement, McCord went back to his office in the blackest of moods. How had it happened that suddenly his whole team was under threat? Heppie had happened, with her officiousness and interference in McCord's little fiefdom; a fiefdom that he had quietly built while Gilchrist was busy planning his next TV appearance and the weekend's game of golf. A horror vision formed in his mind; Sutton gone, Calderwood and Dharwan in a disciplinary, and Amy... it didn't bear thinking about, and he was powerless to prevent any of it.

He picked up his jacket. Maybe the Friday curry-and-chess night with his dad would take his mind off Hepburn.

On his way out of the building, McCord was accosted by Carruthers, the duty sergeant, who always insisted on a chat about how disappointing the weather was for July or any other month that happened to be on the calendar.

"Oh, by the way, sir, did Struthers tell you about" –
Carruthers consulted his visitors' log – "Amanda Jackson?
She came to see you a wee while ago, but you were busy.
Struthers spoke to her."

"Is he still here?" McCord asked.

"No, he clocked off straight afterwards."

"And he didn't leave a note?" McCord asked, although
he knew the answer.

"Can't have been important," Carruthers opined. "He
said she was waffling on, and he was too busy to chat to
attention-seeking women."

McCord's nostrils flared, but he managed to keep his
voice even. "Do you have her contact details?"

"Yes, hang on… here they are."

Carruthers scribbled an address and phone number on
a piece of paper and handed it to McCord.

"Thanks, Jack."

McCord stuffed the note in his pocket and pushed the
door open. He was already late, and he was not going to
cancel again. Amanda Jackson would have to wait.

* * *

Amy's day had not been any better than McCord's. She
had been restless and bad-tempered, and by nine thirty,
she knew she would be unable to sleep. Not being
involved in a murder investigation was intolerable, so she
had decided to stick her long but beautifully shaped nose
into Ross Cartwright's life again to see if she could sniff
anything out.

She wondered if she could call Calderwood at this time,
but surely, on a Friday night he would still be up.

He answered her call after five rings. "Everything okay,
Amy?" he asked, sounding worried.

"Yes, sorry to trouble you," Amy said. "Do you
remember the name of the place Ross Cartwright works
in?"

There was a pause.

"It's Freddy's. Why? You're not thinking of going to a late-night bar to chat up our main suspect? As far as we know, he pushed his wife down a cliff and drove her lover off the road!"

"I'm not meeting him in some dark alleyway," Amy said. "He doesn't know me, there'll be lots of people around, and I'm only going to ask some very innocent questions."

"Is Douglas with you at least?"

"How do you… ach, for God's sake. You and McCord are like two washerwomen! Not that it's any of your business, but Douglas is at a family do tonight."

"Amy, you're not going to Freddy's on your own. Wait."

There was the muffled sound of a quick exchange of words. Amy felt a pang of guilt. Of course, Calderwood was with Dharwan.

"Is Surina there?" Amy asked when the line was clear again. "I'm so sorry."

"It's fine," Calderwood said, and if he was annoyed that the cosy night in with his girlfriend had been interrupted, he did not show it.

"We'll pick you up in an hour. We're practically walking past your flat anyway."

"An hour?" Amy blurted out. It was less than a fifteen-minute walk from Calderwood's place in Stockbridge to Queen Street. But then a thought occurred to her. "I'm so sorry, Duncan," she said again.

Calderwood giggled. "No need to apologise. You're drawing the wrong conclusion. Freddy's doesn't get lively until ten thirty. They're supposed to have very good cocktails there, and Surina wants to doll herself up for the occasion. Have you asked the boss if he wants to come? From what little I remember, we all had a great time when we were last out for cocktails."

Amy's answer came out with greater vehemence than she had intended. "No."

There was a brief silence at the other end. She hoped Calderwood would not start on her and McCord, but he only said, "Ach, I forgot, on Fridays he has a curry with his dad. See you in a bit."

He hung up.

His remark had taken her back to that night when McCord, completely floored by a string of unfamiliar concoctions, had passed out on her sofa, only to be jolted, still hung-over, into the next murder investigation. Happy times. However, things change.

Amy examined her tousled hair and the shadows under her eyes in the bathroom mirror. The colour on her legs had faded, but knee-length was still out of the question. Surina always looked like a princess even without trying, so she'd better make an effort.

Chapter 25

Freddy's was round the corner in Frederick Street, and soon the rectangular white sign above the green wooden door came into view. The party had started, and the muffled beat of dance music seeped out into the street. At the entrance, there was a short queue which was guarded by a bouncer who, to Amy's great disappointment, was not Cartwright. As they shuffled past him, Amy asked, "Is Ross not working tonight?"

The bouncer twiddled with his earpiece. "Sorry, who?"

"Ross Cartwright." Amy batted her eyelids suggestively. "I was hoping to see him tonight."

The bouncer looked her up and down. "Better look elsewhere, miss. He's trouble."

Amy smiled suggestively. "I like a bit of trouble."

The bouncer shook his head disapprovingly. "He's not in and he won't be again."

Amy pretended to be shocked. "Why?"

"Oy!" somebody shouted from the back of the queue. "Move along there at the front, we'd like to get in before midnight!"

The bouncer craned his neck. "It's alright, sir, it'll only take a few minutes!"

It was obvious that he was unwilling to chat any longer, so Amy hurried after Calderwood and Dharwan. Once they had shuffled through the dark, wood-panelled lobby and entered a room called Centre Stage, they hit a wall of noise, the monotonous beat reverberating in their stomachs. Frantically flashing lights cut the people on the dance floor into fragmented, constantly moving shapes. Fortunately, Calderwood led them to a quieter room at the back away from the din, where they could communicate without screaming.

As they perused the cocktail menu, Amy shuddered to think what this spontaneous outing of hers would cost, especially for Dharwan, who was on the modest salary of a police constable. Dharwan, however, looked serene as always while she was dithering between a tequila and a gin-based cocktail.

Amy insisted on paying for the first round and went up to the bar that sported a white neon sign with the message 'Show me the money!'

While the bartender got mixing, Amy leaned casually on the counter, reading the name tag on the bartender's shirt. "I was hoping to speak to Ross tonight, Dylan. Is he not in yet?"

"Ross Cartwright?" he asked.

"Yes, that's him. Ross and I go back a long way. He used to work for me. I was hoping to give him some moral support after all he's been through."

Dylan opened a bottle of Edinburgh gin.

"He doesn't work here anymore."

Amy was all moral disapproval.

"You're not saying he was fired? He was released without charge! Innocent until proven guilty, I'd say!"

Dylan poured a measure into a bulbous glass big enough to crown a kitten.

"That's exactly what the boss said when Ross came back asking for more shifts. He was supposed to be on tonight, but he was barely in the door when one of the guys joked that he would like to do away with his wife himself and get away with it." Dylan shook his head at the stupidity of the remark. "Of course, Ross punched him squarely in the face. The boss came and fired Ross on the spot saying he'd had his chance, but he'd assaulted a member of his staff, and was damaging the reputation of the club. Ross was in such a rage, they had to carry him outside, and he was shouting that he'd pay this guy Slater back for destroying his life."

He took a tray with shaved cucumber, apple slices, strawberries and mint leaves out of a small fridge below the counter and began adding them to the cocktails.

"Did your boss call the police?" Amy asked.

"I don't think so. He said it was punishment enough for Ross to lose his job because he probably wouldn't get another one in the city."

"What did you think of Ross?" Amy asked.

Dylan finished off the cocktails with tonic water and Prosecco and stuck a half-slice of lime on the rim of Amy's drink.

"Ross? I thought he was okay, but... but what with his missus getting murdered and him arrested for the car crash as well, everybody started wondering..."

Amy nodded gravely. "Naturally."

He pushed the card reader towards Amy.

"Cheers," he said, seeing Amy add a generous tip.

Amy returned to the table with the drinks and relayed the conversation to Calderwood and Dharwan, whose forehead was creasing into a frown.

"I'm so sorry to have dragged you out for nothing, Surina," Amy said. "I was hoping… actually, I don't know what I was expecting. It was not so much a long shot as a launch into space."

"No," Dharwan said, "that's not it. I'm worried about what Cartwright might do. No job, notorious now in the whole of Edinburgh – he must be desperate. And desperate people can be dangerous."

"Slater is safe in the Infirmary," Calderwood said. "Turner will be watching him like a hawk, especially since Cartwright was released."

"I still think the boss should know," Dharwan said.

"You're right." Calderwood pulled out his phone and touched a speed dial button.

McCord answered almost immediately. "Calderwood? What's up?"

"Sorry to interrupt your curry night, sir, but we are at the bar where Cartwright was working."

"Who is we?"

Calderwood shot a glance at Amy. "Surina, Amy and I," he said. "I've put you on speaker phone."

There was a brief pause during which Amy wondered if McCord was feeling left out.

But all he said, was, "Ah. And?"

"Cartwright was fired this evening and made threats against Slater. You might want to warn Turner to be especially vigilant tonight," said Calderwood.

"Bloody hell!"

"Pardon, sir?"

The line went dead.

Less than a minute later, Calderwood's phone rang.

"I've sent Turner and another officer to Slater's place," McCord told them.

"Would Turner not be better watching Slater at the hospital?" Calderwood asked.

"Slater discharged himself about an hour ago."

"What?" Amy exclaimed. "Surely, he's not well enough!"

There was another silence. Then McCord's voice was back.

"Turner tried to persuade him to stay put, but Slater said he was feeling much better and wanted to go home. His girlfriend was there, and he said he needed some privacy to talk to her."

"That could well be true," Amy said. "He does have a lot of explaining to do. But he needs protection, whatever he might think."

McCord sounded stung. "Turner phoned me immediately, but I couldn't force Slater to stay in hospital with a protection officer. However, now that Cartwright has made an explicit threat, the situation has changed... And there's something else. When Turner left, the receptionist told him that there had been a disturbance at the main entrance earlier tonight. A big guy with a beard, who was under the influence, had kicked off when a nurse stopped him from entering. They didn't call us because the guy eventually left on his own accord. I bet that was Cartwright."

"The whole thing seems odd, though," Calderwood said. "I mean, Slater discharging himself so suddenly, so late in the day. Why would he do that? He wouldn't have known about Cartwright trying to get into the hospital, but he knew that we weren't able to keep him in custody. So, why not stay where he was safe?"

"Maybe he had less faith in us than we deserve," McCord said. "And there's more."

Calderwood laughed. "Seems I missed all the action by not working overtime."

"That'll teach you," McCord said. "See what you make of that: Turner says Slater had a visit from Amanda Jackson."

Calderwood looked quizzically at Amy and Dharwan.

"Jackson? What did she want with Slater?"

"No idea," McCord said. "Maybe she warned him about Cartwright. She told us she thought he was capable of anything, remember?"

"She was Sarah's best friend," Amy butted in. "She might have wanted to speak to somebody who was grieving for Sarah as well. Exchange stories, memories, you know."

"There must have been more to it than that," McCord said. "Jackson came to the station tonight, but as luck would have it, it was Struthers who spoke to her. He went off duty and didn't leave a note. I've been trying to phone him but he's not picking up. Neither is Jackson. That moron Struthers is doing my head in!"

They heard the insistent buzz of another call coming in.

"That's Turner," McCord said.

The line went quiet. Seconds later, McCord was back.

"There's been a 999 call from Slater's place. I'm off. I'll keep you posted."

McCord hung up.

Calderwood looked at Dharwan, torn in his loyalties.

"I'm sorry, but I have to go."

He grabbed his jacket and rushed out into the street. Amy and Dharwan, hampered by their high heels, tried their best to catch up.

He waved down a taxi, which slowly approached the kerb to disgorge more of Freddy's clients.

"You take this one," he said to Amy and Dharwan. "Make sure you both get home safely. I'll take the next one."

"You must be joking," Amy said, sliding into the back. "We're all going. Surina, get in."

Dharwan smiled at Calderwood, and all his objections melted away.

"Eskbank," he told the driver. "As fast as possible."

Chapter 26

McCord's taxi came to an abrupt halt outside Slater's villa, an oddly shaped modern building with huge front windows. There were two police cars parked in front. Inside one of them sat Cartwright, head down, hands cuffed, watched closely by two constables; one sitting beside him, one standing by the open door. Turner was nowhere to be seen.

McCord flicked open his ID, but it was not necessary. He was well known even in the outskirts of Edinburgh. The constable straightened up.

"Good evening, sir."

"What's happened?"

"We were the first to answer the 999 call," the constable said. "The girlfriend said somebody had forced their way into the house. When we arrived, the colleagues were already on the scene. Mr Cartwright had been trying to strangle Mr Slater and put up quite a fight when Turner arrested him. It took three of us to get him into the car afterwards. Turner said to wait for you before we take him to the station."

McCord bent down to Cartwright, who sat slumped forward.

"Gotcha."

He watched them drive off and swerve to avoid a taxi that came screeching round the corner. His heart skipped a beat when he saw that there were four people inside. He registered with some glee that Amy had not brought her pastry chef on the evening out.

"Going out with two ladies at the same time is definitely breaching the code of conduct," he said to Calderwood, who staggered slightly as he got out of the taxi. "And why has your face turned such an unattractive shade of green?"

"That taxi driver was worse than you behind the wheel," Calderwood mumbled. "I'll never tell them that I'm a police officer in a hurry again."

"Rookie mistake," McCord said.

He swallowed hard as he watched Amy coming towards him in her long, tight-fitting dress, with Dharwan in an elegant, embroidered smock at her side.

"PC Dharwan, your commitment to your job is commendable, but this is going above and beyond. Miss Thornton, I'm surprised you were sensible enough to take some backup with you before interviewing a murder suspect. The mind boggles."

Amy glanced at Calderwood, who was greedily sucking in the fresh evening air and clearly not listening.

"Shall we go in and give our hero of the night a helping hand?" said McCord and stepped past the constable guarding the door into the hall.

It was empty, apart from a staircase leading up to the first floor and two large, pink suitcases. McCord, however, was more interested in the bloodstains on the tiled floor.

"I thought Cartwright tried to strangle Slater," McCord said with a frown, "not stab him."

"He did," said Turner who was joining them from what McCord guessed was the living room.

McCord looked at him, aghast.

"Gee, what happened to you, Turner?"

Turner's left eye was reduced to a thin slit surrounded by swollen, red tissue, his nose was slightly askew, and the insides of his nostrils were caked in blood. He was walking with a slight limp.

"Cartwright wouldn't come quietly," Turner said. "Thank God, I had him down and cuffed by the time Ms Dunbar came back from the kitchen with a frying pan." He leaned in closer and whispered, "I'm not sure which one of them she would have bashed on the head if I hadn't stopped her."

"Why is the ambulance not here yet?" McCord asked.

"Mr Slater said there was no need."

"I meant for you," McCord said. "Otherwise, your nose will never be the same again. Get the constable at the door to drive you to A&E and then home unless they keep you in. Stay at home tomorrow. If I need you to give a formal statement, I'll call you. Off you go. Well done, Turner, very well done."

Turner's battered face beamed.

"Thank you, sir."

McCord and Calderwood, followed by Amy and Dharwan, entered the room Turner had come out of. It was a bright, spacious lounge with a wooden floor offset by light-grey walls and a pristine white suite. A purple orchid was the only splash of colour in the room.

Slater shot up from the sofa to greet the detectives.

"DI McCord! DS Calderwood!" His voice was croaky, and he looked pale. He took in Calderwood's fashionable jeans and McCord's chinos and jumper. "You are off duty! I am so sorry, DI McCord, I should have listened to your advice. If it hadn't been for PC Turner…"

He broke off to clear his throat and turned to Dharwan.

"I almost didn't recognise you there, PC Dharwan. You look as if you had other plans tonight, as well. I'm so sorry."

"No problem, sir," Dharwan replied. "We were worried about you and wanted to check that you and Ms Dunbar were alright. Are you sure you don't want to see a doctor about your throat?"

"Thank you for your concern, but no. I've seen enough doctors to last me a lifetime. And Amy, you are here as well…"

He cleared his throat again and took a sip from the glass of water in front of him. "Yvonne, would you get our guests something to drink?"

Yvonne Dunbar was dressed in silk trousers and high-heeled shoes. After the excitement of the evening, she must have touched up her make-up and brushed her hair. As she sat on the armchair, she looked like a celebrity in *Hello!* magazine. At Slater's words, she rose without a smile and disappeared into the kitchen.

Slater followed her with his eyes. "It's been quite a night."

"I know your throat is still sore, but it would be very helpful if you could give us an account of what exactly happened tonight," Calderwood said. "Even if Cartwright was caught in the act, we still need to write a report. If you don't mind, I'll take notes on my phone."

"Not at all," Slater said. "And please make sure you mention PC Turner's outstanding bravery, and the other constable as well. Apart from that, there is not much to tell. Yvonne and I… well, we were having a chat about our future, and she was very upset and about to leave. Cartwright must have been waiting outside watching the house, because when Yvonne opened the front door, he pushed past her and went for me."

His voice broke. He picked up his glass and gulped down more of the water before he was able to continue. "He was so strong; I couldn't do anything. When he had his hands round my neck, I thought I was a goner, but then PC Turner arrived; no idea how he got here so quickly. Did you still have him watch me?" he asked McCord, who shook his head.

"No, but fortunately for you, DS Calderwood told me that Cartwright had been sacked tonight and made threats against you, so I sent PC Turner to check up on you. Just as well."

"You can say that again. He saved my life. When I met Cartwright at the station, he was aggressive, but I had no idea he was such a maniac."

"Didn't Amanda Jackson warn you about him when she visited you this afternoon?" McCord asked.

Slater began to cough, clearly struggling to breathe.

"She did," Slater said eventually, "but I didn't take her seriously. What a fool I've been!"

Yvonne returned from the kitchen with glasses, a bottle of wine and a carton of juice. She set the tray down heavily, making the glasses clink.

An awkward silence ensued while Yvonne poured Amy, Dharwan and Calderwood a glass of pinot grigio and McCord an orange juice. Slater sipped his water, grimacing each time he swallowed.

"I'm leaving now," Yvonne said to McCord, "unless…"

"Once you've given your statement to the constable at the door, you are free to go, of course," McCord said, "but it is very late. Do you have somewhere to go?"

"Don't worry, I'll be fine," she said and went out into the hall, slamming the door.

McCord pensively regarded the trembling frame.

"Is this about the paternity test by any chance?"

Calderwood shot McCord a glance as if to say, 'Really?', while Amy closed her eyes.

Slater sat very still, breathing heavily.

"It was positive," he whispered. "I am the boy's father."

"One day at a time," Dharwan said with a smile. "A year from now you probably won't be able to remember how you managed without him in your life."

Slater grimaced.

"Maybe she'll come round," Amy said. "She needs time."

Slater lowered his head. "You know, you were right about the money. When I won those millions, I thought my life would be fantastic, but they've been a curse."

"Now that Cartwright is out of circulation, you can have a fresh start," Amy said. "With or without Yvonne. And there is still your brother who cares about you. He's the only family you've got, well… apart from Riley, of course."

Slater took another careful sip of his water and said nothing.

Amy laid a comforting hand on his arm.

"You haven't quite taken it in, but the nightmare is over. You can finally start the life you have always dreamed of. As soon as you're better, you'll have to give me an exclusive, though," she said with a cheeky grin. "I think it's only fair if I sacrificed my evening out to rescue you."

Everybody laughed; even Slater attempted a smile. "Fair enough, I suppose," he said.

"How about me bringing some sandwiches for a working lunch tomorrow?" Amy asked. "It'll do you good to have some company and to get everything off your chest."

Slater shook his head in disbelief.

"You're something else, you know that? But okay," he said.

Amy raised her glass.

"Cheers. To new beginnings!"

"Cheers," echoed the others.

* * *

Twenty minutes later, Dharwan and Amy were about to get into the taxi that was to take them home when Calderwood took McCord aside.

"Now would be a good time," he said with a wink.

McCord hesitated, and by the time he made a move, Amy had settled in the back seat next to Dharwan.

"Too late," McCord said with a distinct feeling of relief. "Thanks for coming out, Calderwood," he said. "It all turned out well in the end. Heppie should be happy."

Calderwood chuckled.

"Mind you, Dunbar might well make a complaint about Turner arriving when he did. By the sound of their argument, I bet she'd been much happier if Cartwright had managed to finish the job."

Chapter 27

It was a very subdued Cartwright who sat opposite McCord and Calderwood in Interview Room 1 the next morning. All fight had left that big, strong frame, and he seemed to have shrunk overnight. Straight after his arrest the previous evening, he had called his lawyer, who had advised him not to say a single word until he arrived there in the morning.

"I hope you have been treated well in custody?" the lawyer asked Cartwright, who nodded impassively. "There are bruises and a cut on your face."

"Mr Cartwright sustained those minor injuries while two of my officers were preventing him from strangling Mr Daniel Slater," McCord said, grimly. "After the ensuing fight, one of these officers needed hospital treatment for a broken nose and a knee injury. The relevant witness statements will be shared with the defence in due course."

The lawyer nodded, gravely.

"The facts of this case are not in question," McCord continued. "Mr Cartwright caused a disturbance at the hospital yesterday when he was refused access to Mr Slater. He then turned up for his shift at Freddy's, assaulted a member of staff and was promptly fired. After a spell in The Jolly Judge – you couldn't make it up, DS Calderwood, could you? – where Mr Cartwright consumed a copious amount of alcohol, he took a taxi to Mr Slater's house, where he lay in wait outside the door. When Mr Slater's girlfriend opened the door, he forced his way in and proceeded to strangle Mr Slater, who was standing in the hallway. He would have succeeded if two police officers had not arrived at the scene and prevented a murder."

"Hang on, DI McCord," the lawyer interrupted. "You are straying from the facts into your personal prejudice against my client. Murder implies malicious forethought. He was very drunk, as you yourself pointed out, and highly emotional after being fired. Where is the proof that he was waiting outside?"

McCord cursed him silently. He needed Cartwright to feel afraid in order to get a confession out of him for Sarah Cartwright's murder, and this bleeding-heart liberal was not helping.

"We're still trying to contact the taxi driver who took him to Mr Slater's house," he said. "He will be able to confirm the time of his arrival, and we know the precise time of the attack."

"Well, let's wait for that confirmation before we make any assumptions."

The lawyer made a note of that before he continued.

"Also, you are suggesting that someone intent on committing a murder would take a taxi there, whose driver could easily identify him in court. That does not sound very credible to me. Did Mr Slater need medical treatment after the attack?"

"His larynx was damaged, and I encouraged him to see a doctor—"

"But you yourself have no medical training, do you?"

"No," McCord admitted with clenched teeth.

"I understand that Mr Slater was under protection while he was at the hospital," the lawyer said, looking through his notes.

"Yes. After an attempt on his life, I'd say this was appropriate, wouldn't you?"

The lawyer ignored the question. "But when Mr Slater discharged himself, he declined a protection officer?"

"Against my advice," McCord said.

"It shows, however, that Mr Slater was not particularly afraid of my client, wouldn't you agree?"

"His judgement must have been impaired by the head injury he sustained in the crash."

"You are straying once again into the realms of medical speculation, DI McCord," the lawyer said. "So, we are down to common assault with diminished responsibility, I'd say. Wouldn't you agree?"

"No, I wouldn't," McCord snapped. "This attempted murder is the third crime we believe Mr Cartwright has committed. Motivated by pathological jealousy, for which we have several witnesses, Mr Cartwright killed his wife Sarah by pushing her off the Salisbury Crags, and then attempted to kill Mr Slater, who was her lover, first by forcing him off the road, and when Mr Slater survived that, he went to his home to strangle him. Do you want to get him off so that he can try for the third time?"

The lawyer did not look perturbed.

"Unless you have unearthed new evidence, we have to assume that Mr Cartwright had nothing to do with his wife's murder, nor Mr Slater's car accident. We have only Mr Slater's word that it was my client who forced him off the road, and, as you say yourself, his judgement might well have been impaired."

McCord made a fist under the table. "For the moment, we are only charging him with the attempted murder of Mr Daniel Slater, because that's what it was. And before you ask, he will remain in custody until he is due to appear in court."

McCord leaned forward and waited until Ross Cartwright lifted his head and looked him in the eyes. "I fully intend to make the murder and the other attempted murder charges stick, Mr Cartwright, so think carefully how you plead. Because if you show no remorse and no consideration towards the victim and her loved ones, you will go down for life, and in your case, it will mean life."

Cartwright swallowed hard.

"I didn't kill me wife," he said quietly. "I loved her."

"Interview terminated at 10.22," McCord said.

Calderwood pressed the stop button and led Cartwright down to the cells.

The lawyer rose.

"I've heard a lot about you, DI McCord," he said. "You even risk your own life to put the bad guys away. Believe it or not, I understand your frustration. It may all seem very straightforward to you, but you need to prove beyond reasonable doubt that Cartwright committed those other crimes, and it is my job to make sure that you do."

He held out his hand and McCord shook it.

"I hope you can solve Sarah Cartwright's murder soon, one way or the other. If it was Cartwright, he needs to go away for a long time. If it wasn't him, he needs this cloud hanging over him lifted, so that he can rebuild his life."

McCord walked slowly back to his office. He should have felt satisfied. He had solved multiple cases and had the perpetrator in custody. If he had no irrefutable evidence, it was not for want of trying. Some just got away. At least, they had prevented another murder; although, if Cartwright had managed to kill Slater, he would have gone to prison for the maximum sentence they could justify. McCord shook off that uncharitable thought and sat heavily on his chair. The euphoria that usually came with getting the bad guy did not come. Justice would not be done. And Sandhu's murder remained unsolved without even a credible suspect left.

There was a hesitant knock on the open door, and a downcast Turner entered. A thick plaster was stuck on his nose, and he was still limping.

"Turner, what on earth are you doing here? I told you to take the day off."

"I'm fine," Turner said. "I came in to look through the CCTV again before the report goes off to the procurator fiscal. After last night, I wanted Cartwright off our streets for good."

"I thought Struthers had checked every camera between the station and along Old Dalkeith Road," McCord said. "There is no coverage."

"But," Turner said, "he didn't check the surrounding area. The last time Cartwright's car was picked up it was going past the Royal Infirmary. After that, there are only two major junctions before the accident spot. So, if we can show that he didn't turn off Old Dalkeith Road, it proves that he drove past the site of the accident at the right time."

McCord sat up and banged his fist on the table.

"And Struthers didn't think of that? What's he been doing all this time, having a wee nap?" He took a deep breath. "Never mind, I'll deal with him later. What have you found?"

Turner hung his head.

"You won't like it, sir."

"Come on, out with it."

"I've got Cartwright on CCTV two minutes before the accident He had turned off into Ferniehill Drive and was caught on camera again on Captain's Road at the time of the accident. So, it wasn't him."

"What?!"

"Sorry, sir, I so wanted to nail him," Turner said. "All those hours of trawling CCTV, and then I find proof that he didn't do it!"

McCord shook his head.

"Nonsense, you've done a great job. At least we know something for sure, even if it isn't what we wanted to find. Go and put it on the incident board. I need to think about this one."

Turner hobbled off.

As McCord leant back in his seat, something rustled in his trouser pocket. He pulled out a scrunched-up note. Amanda Jackson. What with all the drama the night before, he had completely forgotten about her. Why had she come to the station yesterday? He smoothed out the piece of paper and called her number again.

It rang for ages. He was about to give up when a suspicious voice answered, "Hello?"

"DI McCord from St Leonard's," he said quickly before she could change her mind and hang up. "You came to the station yesterday. I've tried to phone you a couple of times."

He tried to keep the accusation out of his tone.

"I told your colleague everything last night," she said, "Stutters, or something like that. When you called, I thought, like, someone had got the wrong number."

"Never mind," McCord said. "Could you tell me again what it was you wanted to say? DS Struthers' message wasn't... very clear."

"No wonder. He wasn't listening at all. Too busy trying to impress one of your women PCs, like. We think we've got rid of those dinosaurs, and then–"

"Yes, yes, Ms Jackson," McCord interrupted what he feared would be a lengthy tirade. "What was it you wanted to tell us?"

Jackson huffed. "I thought I'd go and see this lover of Sarah's. I was her best friend, like, and I just can't understand why she would keep all those secrets from me." She sounded as if she was about to cry.

"And?" McCord asked.

"What do you mean, 'and'?"

McCord tried to remain patient.

"Have you got a theory why Sarah Cartwright didn't mention her affair to you?"

"It was weird, like," she said, then ground to a halt again.

McCord was beginning to lose the will to live.

"What exactly do you mean by 'weird'?"

"Well, when I asked how they had met, like, he told me that he chatted her up in a cocktail bar, like, and after three gin and tonics she agreed to see him again."

She paused again, clearly expecting a response.

"So?" McCord asked, deciding to end the call at the next opportunity.

"Sarah never ever drank gin. It made her cry. Which is also weird, like, 'cause, normally, gin cheers people up, doesn't it?"

McCord stroked his chin. A terrible thought sneaked into his brain and bounced about like a rubber ball gone mad, but before he could catch it, Jackson was speaking again.

"And when we were talking about her, like, sharing stories and memories, he didn't seem to have any to share. He didn't know anything about her degree, like, and believe me, she told everybody, and I mean everybody, about it because she was so proud of the letters after her name. I remember thinking at the time–"

"That he wasn't her boyfriend at all," McCord finished her sentence.

"Yes," Jackson said. "But why–"

"Thanks."

McCord hung up.

Slater hadn't been Sarah Cartwright's lover. He hardly knew her.

McCord was still trying to get the ideas whirring round his head into some sort of meaningful order when Calderwood breezed into the office.

"That's Cartwright safely stowed away," said Calderwood. "Pity he didn't budge on the murder but who knows what a prolonged spell in a cell is going to do. Do you want me to prepare the paperwork for the procurator fiscal? I think we should play safe and get him on the assault; that's better than–"

"Sit down, Calderwood. The paperwork can wait. What would you say if I told you that Slater never was Sarah Cartwright's lover?"

Calderwood stared at McCord.

"Never…? Why would he lie about that, and why would he pay her all that money?"

"Exactly my thought," McCord said.

Calderwood's eyes widened. "Blackmail?"

"Maybe." McCord jumped up and began pacing up and down the office. "That would explain why she didn't tell her best friend. But what could she have been blackmailing him about?"

Calderwood frowned. "Something he did in the past… but what secrets would he be hiding that made him vulnerable to blackmail? By all accounts, he is Mr Nice Guy!"

"Maybe they weren't *his* secrets; maybe they were somebody else's, someone close to him," McCord said.

Calderwood brightened up. "Of course, Amy said that Richard McAllister felt guilty about something. Maybe Slater was protecting his little brother?"

"He doesn't seem to like McAllister much, though," McCord said. "Why would he pay all this money to help him?" He scratched his head. "I need to speak to that social worker."

Calderwood was looking at him with a half-smile.

"I know, I know, I should have listened to Amy," McCord grumbled. "Just get me his contact details. And then start on the Cartwright report."

Chapter 28

Amy was woken up by a noise that dragged her from the deepest recesses of her unconscious. It took her a while to realise that it was her doorbell chiming. It had been past three o'clock in the morning when she had finally fallen asleep after all the excitement of the previous evening. Who would come to see her in the middle of the night? She looked at her phone that was lying on the bedside table. Quarter to twelve! She jumped out of bed.

The bell rang again. Probably the postman, lazy sod. Or maybe her mum was working in her boutique downstairs and needed some milk for her coffee.

"Coming!"

She flung on her dressing gown and padded across the corridor. Without looking through the spyhole, she opened the door and gave a start. Standing only inches away was Richard McAllister sticking a bunch of flowers into her face. Instinctively, she pulled back, and by the time she had recovered from the shock and given up fixing her dishevelled hair, he was standing in the hallway.

"I've come to take you out for lunch," he said, taking in her appearance. "I'm sorry I dragged you out of bed. I thought you'd be up and about by now. Good night last night, was it?"

"That's one way of putting it," Amy said. "Ross Cartwright tried to strangle your brother–"

"What?!"

"But" – she held her arms up in a calming gesture – "he's fine, and Cartwright is in custody. The police came just in time."

"Wow," McAllister said. "Thank God." After a second's pause, he added, "Has Cartwright confessed to his wife's murder yet?"

A little warning bell jingled in Amy's brain. She shouldn't be telling McAllister about the case. But then, his brother had almost been killed. She decided she needed caffeine before saying or doing anything else.

"Coffee?"

"That'd be great, thanks," McAllister said.

Turning her back to him, she led the way to the kitchen.

* * *

After ending the call to Graham Knight, McCord lowered his phone, deep in thought. Calderwood looked expectantly at him. "And? What did he say?"

McCord's eyes were fixed on the orange wall. "I think we got it wrong about the blackmail."

"It wasn't about something Richard McAllister had done?"

"Not likely. The blackmail was about Slater. It's been staring us in the face, Calderwood! What's the greatest thing that's ever happened to Slater?"

"Him winning the lottery," Calderwood said. "But what do you think he did? Forged the ticket? Don't the organisers check very carefully that the win is legit? How could he have cheated?"

"Good point. And the other question is: how did Sarah Cartwright know about it? If they weren't lovers, where is the link?"

Calderwood shrugged. "Nothing came up in the investigation."

"We weren't looking for a link because we thought we knew what it was. Get me Sarah's notebook from the evidence store, will you?"

Calderwood hurried off.

McCord googled Slater's name and lottery win. He wrote down the winning numbers and examined the photos of a beaming Yvonne Dunbar next to Slater, whose smile was strained. "You didn't want your win to be made public, did you?" McCord asked the picture on the screen. Then he read the article underneath.

"There you go, sir." Out of breath, Calderwood put Sarah Cartwright's notebook on McCord's desk.

"There's something not quite right about this," McCord said.

"What?"

He swivelled the screen round so that Calderwood could see.

"The actual draw was on 23 February, but Slater didn't claim the prize until 3 May. It says here that he had mislaid the ticket. How long does it take to rifle through your pockets and drawers to find a ticket that's worth millions of pounds?"

McCord picked up Sarah Cartwright's notebook and flicked through its pages.

"Here they are," he said triumphantly, holding open the page next to the numbers she had scribbled down. 4 5 9 15 26 31 + 5 3. Underlined, twice. Sarah Cartwright must have listened to the lottery draw and written down the numbers. Could the winning ticket have been hers?"

"No, that doesn't make sense," Calderwood said. "Look there, on the previous page, there is a date, 1 May. She must have written the numbers down after that."

McCord nodded. "She wrote them down when she read or heard about Slater winning the jackpot because she noticed something. Why did she cross them out one by one? Something must have told her that Slater had cheated."

"But Slater can't have stolen the ticket. Don't they check with the outlet where the ticket was handed in?"

"They do," McCord said. "But they can't identify who bought the ticket, nor who it was bought for."

Calderwood frowned.

"You mean he bought it for somebody else? But why did that person not come forward?"

"Why indeed?" McCord said with a grim smile.

"You don't think…" Calderwood sat down. "Oh, my God."

"That's exactly what I do think. What kind of people need others to buy their stuff for them?"

"Old people? Disabled people?"

"Exactly. I need Sutton. Now."

* * *

It took Sutton only a few minutes to pull the employment records of Sarah Cartwright and Daniel Slater. They had worked for the same company offering private home care, and among their patients one name cropped up twice: a Dr Margaret Curran, resident in Vanburgh Place. McCord felt a sudden wave of nausea.

"Tell me about her," he said in a compressed voice.

Sutton's fingertips flew over the keyboard.

"Born April 23rd, 1940, died February 23rd this year, never married, no children. PhD on the applications of pi in engineering. Maths lecturer at Edinburgh University, retired August 2000."

McCord looked at the numbers of the lottery draw he had written on a Post-it note. Normally, one used significant numbers; birthdays, children's birthdays, addresses…

"Where did she live before Vanburgh Place?"

"Born there," Sutton croaked.

"What do you make of this?" he asked her, sticking the Post-it note on her desk. "I think they might be her lottery numbers. Any ideas?"

Sutton glanced at the number before her gaze fastened on the third button down on McCord's shirt.

"Pi, in a different order," she said.

McCord bounced up and down, barely able to control the urge to shower her with praise. "Could you hack the National Lottery computers for me and check where this ticket was bought? I don't have time to go through the official channels."

Before he had even finished the sentence, Sutton had turned back to her computer. She seemed to have forgotten that he was there, so he stayed and watched her quietly. Until he had confirmation of his suspicion, he would not be able to do or think about anything else, anyway.

A few minutes later, Sutton turned the screen towards him.

McCord bent down to read. His heart was about to burst with excitement, sadness, anger and fear, all at once.

"Thank you, DC Sutton," he mumbled and hastily weaved out of the den.

Outside, Calderwood was waiting for him. "And?"

"Later," McCord said, moving towards the door. "Get me Yvonne Dunbar on the phone. I need to speak to her."

McCord pulled out his own phone and pressed speed dial. There was no answer. Frantic now, he shouted at Calderwood to follow him to the car park.

They ran downstairs, Calderwood trying in vain to get McCord to tell him what was going on.

In the car, McCord fastened his phone to the dashboard and dialled the number again. This time, he got through.

"Amy?" he shouted breathlessly, "are you alright?"

"Of course, I am," came the answer. "I was about to call you. You'll never believe what Richard has told me."

"I know," McCord said. "Is he with you?"

"Yes, we were just—"

"Stay where you are, both of you."

"But—"

He hung up.

Calderwood pressed the loudspeaker icon on his phone and held it closer to McCord. "Yvonne Dunbar."

"Ms Dunbar," McCord said. "Do you have any idea where your boyfriend is now?"

"My ex-boyfriend," she said pointedly. "I can tell you exactly where he is. The departure lounge at the airport, the swine. Why are you asking?"

"Which airline?" McCord asked, ignoring her question.

"I don't know but I found a ticket to Geneva in his desk yesterday. A single, one-way ticket." She paused to let the implications of this sink in. "He is going to live the high life in Switzerland. Without me. That's why I left yesterday. I couldn't stay one minute longer in the same house as that…"

McCord had stopped listening; he was executing a highly illegal U-turn. He raced off towards the west of the city. Once the honking of horns had subsided, he mouthed to Calderwood to alert the airport authorities.

Calderwood nodded and swapped the phones.

"Ms Dunbar," McCord said, cutting short a string of expletives, "where were you on 2 March?"

Dunbar was momentarily speechless.

"Are you asking me for an alibi for something?" she asked angrily.

"Just answer my question," McCord said.

"I can't remember, can I? Do you know where you were on a certain day more than four months ago?"

McCord felt uncomfortable at the thought that he might do. Either at the station or at home or at his dad's for their curry night if it was a Friday.

"Could you please check straightaway?"

"Wait, it'll be in my diary," Dunbar said.

For a while, there was only low muttering at the other end. Then her voice returned. "Oh yeah, here we are. I remember now. I was in Newcastle for a hen do."

"And Mr Slater wasn't with you then?"

"Of course not," she scoffed. "It was a *hen* do!"

"Thank you."

He touched the red icon.

Calderwood had also finished his call. "There was a flight that left for Geneva via Amsterdam two hours ago. They're checking if he was on it. The boarding for the next direct flight starts in twenty minutes. If he's still at the airport, he won't get on that plane."

"Unless he has a fake passport," McCord said. "Send them a picture."

After that was done, Calderwood turned to McCord, who was staring at the road, gripping the steering wheel tightly, willing the other cars to go faster.

"Are you going to tell me what the hell is going on?" Calderwood asked.

And so, McCord did.

Chapter 29

As they ran into the check-in hall of Edinburgh airport, McCord expected to be met with the airport security staff. What he did not expect, was Amy rushing towards him with a bewildered-looking Richard McAllister in tow.

"What are you two doing here?" McCord burst out.

"Nice to see you, too," Amy said. "If you'd listened to me for once, I could have saved you some time. After Richard had told me, we drove straight to Dan's house. I thought it would be the ideal opportunity to get those two to make up. Dan wasn't there, but one of his nosey neighbours had seen him getting into a taxi with a large suitcase telling the driver to take him to the airport. What is going on?"

A burly man in uniform stepped forward.

"DI McCord? If you follow me, we have detained Daniel Slater in the British Airways departure lounge."

They threaded their way through the lines of passengers patiently waiting for their check-in queue to move forward.

In a small office, guarded by a security detail, Daniel Slater was sitting on a plastic chair. He rose when McCord came into the room followed by his little entourage.

"Don't you think this is a bit over the top, DI McCord? I'd have been happy to help you with your inquiries when I returned from my holiday."

His expression hardened when he saw Richard McAllister enter the room, his face one big question mark.

"Strange holiday when you only paid for a one-way ticket," McCord pointed out.

"I wasn't sure when I would be back," Slater said. "What do you want? Missing my meeting with Miss Thornton without cancelling was rude, but not a crime. Surely, you haven't come to arrest me."

"As a matter of fact, I have," McCord said.

"You must be joking," Slater said. "Ross Cartwright killed his wife and then tried to kill me twice. The case is closed, and you've got him behind bars. Took you long enough to do that!"

"Ross Cartwright didn't kill his wife, and he didn't force you off the road as you have claimed. You knew all this, of course, because it was you who killed Sarah Cartwright, and when we found no evidence that would convict her husband, you blamed him for your accident to make sure he stayed behind bars. Just out of curiosity, what was it that made you swerve into that field? A deer?"

Slater said nothing.

"Fortunately for Ross Cartwright, a CCTV camera caught him on a completely different road at the time of the crash."

"So, I got it wrong about the accident," Slater said. "After all, I suffered a head injury and temporary loss of memory. But me killing Sarah? That's ridiculous!"

"Nobody is laughing, Mr Slater," McCord said. "Sarah Cartwright recognised the winning lottery numbers because she had taken the same numbers to Jai Sandhu's shop every week while she was looking after Dr Curran. I suspect Dr Curran had told Sarah about pi and her PhD, so when those numbers cropped up after her death, Sarah wrote them down to double-check–"

Slater snorted. "You're making all this up!"

Unperturbed, McCord continued.

"She recognised you as well, from the handover when she left her job as Dr Curran's home carer and passed it on to you. I bet she then visited her only to find out that she had sadly passed away – on the exact day of the lottery draw."

"Poor Margaret died of heart failure," Slater said, but McCord thought he saw a flicker of uncertainty in Slater's eyes. "The doctor said she took too many of her pills. Sadly, she was a little confused at the end."

"And that end happily coincided with her winning 7.8 million in the lottery," McCord said. "On a ticket that you had bought with her money."

"I hope you're not suggesting that I killed her? That's absurd! She even left me something in her will."

"Yes, I've heard that you did quite well out of your old ladies, Mr Slater. I bet they all loved you. But the few hundred pounds here and there were not enough for you, were they? You wanted more. You wanted the jackpot."

McAllister blanched. "Dan," he whispered, "what have you done?"

Slater rose. "Shut up!" he said, then turned to McCord. "I don't have to listen to this garbage. You have been accusing me of two murders in as many minutes without any proof. I'm out of here."

He made for the door.

"Sit down," McCord said in his dangerous quiet voice. "You're not going anywhere. Sarah Cartwright blackmailed you about the ticket. You transferred the money to her twice, but then you took out twenty thousand pounds in cash over a week to hand over to Sarah at the Crags. She suddenly wanted even more, didn't she?"

Slater slid back onto his chair and folded his arms.

"I'm saying nothing more without a lawyer."

McCord shrugged.

"Please yourself," he said. "It doesn't matter. When Sarah went back to find out about Dr Curran, she must have passed Jai Sandhu's former shop. I don't think she made the connection immediately; but eventually, she put two and two together."

Amy gasped. "Sandhu?"

"Yes," McCord said. "Mr Slater here knew that the lottery people would check where the ticket had been bought. Not a problem, you'd think. Unfortunately, Mr Sandhu must have known that he bought the ticket for Dr Curran. Ever since Mr Sandhu took over the shop, she had got her lottery ticket there until her carers had to do it for her. First Sarah Cartwright, and then you, Mr Slater. You wouldn't have wanted to draw attention to her timely death, would you? So, Mr Sandhu had to go before you could claim your prize."

Slater still kept his arms folded, but his whole body had tensed. McCord leaned forward so that his nose almost touched Slater's. "And don't you start about there not being any proof," he said. "I'm sure my sergeant has found out by now where you bought the petrol can and the torch, and we will identify you on the CCTV we have of the arsonist. I knew something wasn't quite right with the re-enactment video, but I couldn't put my finger on it. You have a very peculiar gait, Mr Slater; has anybody told you that? A bit like a ship in rough seas. And that's what you've always been, haven't you? Lost and desperate for love and the good life that was denied you, while your brother had it all!"

Suddenly, Slater jumped up.

"Half-brother," he hissed. "A spoilt little brat, but my mother loved him, not me. Me she hated, and you know why? My father buggered off, and so did Ricky's—"

"How can you say that?" McAllister's voice broke as he fought back tears. "He died in a car crash! He loved Mum, and us—"

"Not me! He left!" Slater shouted. "And her? She drank herself to death, while I did everything. Everything she should have done. I made your meals, I washed your clothes, I got you to school. It didn't matter. She drank, and what did you do? You got yourself into trouble all the time. And when our one chance came, my one chance to get out of all that shit, you blew it!"

Slater fell silent and took a deep breath.

McAllister had stopped crying and was staring at his brother. "Dan, what are you talking about?"

"Don't pretend you don't know," Slater sneered. "After she had turned up drunk at the parents' evening, they sent a social worker round, remember? We could have been taken away there and then, we could have been adopted, got a nice home, nice parents – and what do you do? You tell the social worker it had all been a one-off because of a party, and how wonderful everything is, and that you eat your vegetables and do your homework every day! She believed you and left us there, for another year!"

"I didn't want to leave," McAllister said.

Slater grunted.

"Why would you? I was the one who cleaned up after the pair of you. That was all I was good for."

"No." McAllister stretched out his arm, but Slater recoiled from his touch.

"Dan," McAllister said, "I need to know."

Slater straightened up, his teeth bared. "Don't bullshit me; you've always known, you did your damnedest to get me locked up!"

"So, it's true?" Amy asked.

McCord nodded. "I spoke to Graham Knight earlier."

"He doesn't know anything," Slater spat. "He wasn't there."

"No, but you were, weren't you?" McCord said. "You were at home when your mother had the stroke; you knew, and you did nothing. You just waited, hoping to be finally free."

"It took longer than I thought," Slater said, his voice betraying no emotion. "She couldn't really shout anymore, her whole right-hand side was frozen, but she moaned and drooled; it was disgusting. At long last, she passed out. But then Ricky comes home and calls an ambulance."

McAllister had stopped fighting the tears; they were running down his face as he stared uncomprehendingly at his brother.

"Too late, as it turned out," McCord said. "Luckily for you, your mother died on the way to the hospital without regaining consciousness, and at long last you got to where you wanted to be. Unfortunately, Ricky didn't believe the story that you were busy in the kitchen and hadn't noticed that your mum had a stroke. He knew, or at least suspected, that you had let your mother die, because you hated her, and you hated Ricky as well. Were you not scared he would talk?"

"Oh, he did talk," Slater said scornfully. "He told the counsellor all about it, and Graham Knight as well. I could tell from the way he looked at me afterwards."

"But you didn't get any counselling, did you?" McCord said.

Slater snorted. "I didn't need counselling; I needed a different family. But I got nothing. Story of my life."

"Graham Knight told me," McCord said to McAllister, "that you retracted your accusation after a while. Did you?"

McAllister wiped away the tears, but his voice was still shaky. "The counsellor said that I was understandably angry about my mum's death and that I was projecting my anger onto Dan, that I was looking for a culprit where there was only a tragedy. Eventually, I convinced myself that I had been wrong, and as I got older, I felt terrible; terrible for Dan. Because he is right, I was my mum's favourite, I was incredibly selfish and left everything to him to sort out. And after all that, I accused him of killing our mum and probably scuppered any chance of him being adopted. That's what he was always desperate for: to be adopted. He never stopped watching *David Copperfield* and *Annie*."

"You didn't spoil his chances," McCord said. "Your suspicions never went into your brother's file; there was no way of proving any of it, and up to then, your brother had always been such a good kid. Too good, as it turns out. Anyway, Graham Knight told me that children hardly ever get adopted once they are older than six or seven. You had a rare bit of luck: your adoptive parents were looking for a boy just like you who reminded them of the son they had lost." He turned to Slater. "You went to some nice foster parents, though, didn't you?"

"Nice!" Slater snorted. "They got a kick out of being charitable, and if they hadn't been paid for fostering me, they'd have chucked me out in a heartbeat. I left when I turned sixteen. I knew by then it was only up to me to get what I want. That's the difference: Ricky was loved by Mum, Ricky was adopted, Ricky got an education — he always was the one who was looked after. All I've ever done was caring for people, but now it gave me an opportunity to get close to them. It took so long, I stopped believing I would ever get there. They all went, 'Oh, isn't Dan wonderful', but did they love me enough to leave me their dosh? Nope. Dogs, cats, any do-gooders you can think of, but not me."

"And then Margaret Curran hit the jackpot," McCord said.

There was a mad glint in Slater's eyes. "7.8 million pounds. Are you seriously telling me I should have let the old bat claim it?" He spread his arms wide. "It wasn't just money. It was a new life for me. My new life." He thumped on his chest. "Don't you see? The money was no use to her; in a couple of months, she wouldn't have known what a tenner looked like, never mind what to do with it. The only way for her was down, and she was as good as dead anyway. I did her a favour, just like my mother. They did it to themselves when you think about it."

He looked McCord straight in the eye. "And so did Sarah Cartwright. Who the hell did she think she was, interfering in other people's affairs and blackmailing me?"

"So, you arranged to meet her on top of the Crags to hand over more money?"

"Yes, she couldn't have more going through her accounts without the taxman noticing. If she hadn't been so greedy… it was her own fault."

McCord tried to stay calm. He needed one last confession.

"And Mr Sandhu? Was it his own fault, too, that he choked to death in a fire?" McCord asked.

Slater shrugged.

"I didn't want to kill him, but I had no choice. It was my life or his. And now, after all the sacrifices I've made…"

He groaned.

McCord turned away in disgust.

"Calderwood, read him his rights and get him into the car."

* * *

When Calderwood had led Slater away, McCord shuddered as if trying to shake off the glimpse into the abyss that was Slater's mind. He turned to find Amy looking at him with a strange expression.

"Well done, DI McCord," she said. "Of course, you would have got there more quickly if you had investigated the brothers from the beginning as I suggested."

Instantly, McCord's hackles were up, but then he saw her lips twitching.

"If I had done as you suggested, poor Mandy Jackson would be in jail now," he said. "Although, when I think about it, she is a clear and present danger to the English language."

"You are such a snob!"

McCord marvelled how the corners of her eyes crinkled in amusement, and the sound of her laughter made the darkness disappear.

He swallowed.

"There is something I wanted to ask you," he began.

Her eyes were bright in anticipation. "Yes?"

"My dad and Clare are getting married—"

"How lovely!" Amy exclaimed. "When I met them, I felt that they were so well suited to each other." She giggled. "I suppose it's never too late to find romance."

McCord responded with an uncertain laugh. "Anyway, I was wondering… if you'd come to the wedding." He paused. "As my plus-one. It's very important to my dad… eh, unless that causes problems with your boyfriend," he added.

"Not my boyfriend," Amy said.

McCord felt his airwaves close. "No?"

"He is very sweet…"

"But?"

"I've realised I'm more the savoury type," Amy said.

"So, you will come to the wedding with me?"

Amy smiled.

"Congratulations, McCord. You've got yourself a date."

Chapter 30

St Leonard's seemed to be taking a deep breath before the Saturday night fever would begin. The weekend duty staff were catching up with the latest about the Cartwright and Sandhu cases, with the usual suspects claiming that they had always thought that Slater was a dodgy character.

Calderwood and Dharwan had cleared the incident boards, and McCord saved and filed the report of Daniel Slater's arrest and confession. He was being processed downstairs having been charged with the murders of Margaret Curran, Jai Sandhu and Sarah Cartwright. The odds of getting a conviction for Margaret Curran's murder were close to zero, but McCord felt she deserved to be on the list. The procurator fiscal could always throw out the case if she wanted to.

On the advice of his lawyer, Ross Cartwright had pleaded guilty to two counts of assault, but McCord had agreed to put forward mitigating circumstances from the outset, so he had been released pending his court hearing. McCord suspected that Amy's forthcoming article would turn Cartwright's notoriety into celebrity status, but McCord doubted he would be inclined to cash in on it with a lucrative book deal as others had done before him.

"What's going to happen to Slater's millions now that he is going down for life?" Calderwood asked.

"Since they were the proceeds of crime, I suspect the Crown Office will nab them," McCord said. "But seeing that he has a dependent child, Kimberley MacLean might have a case for a generous settlement for Riley. And once she's sold her story to the papers, she'll be quids in."

Calderwood picked up his jacket. "Surina, Turner and I are going for a celebratory drink. Are you coming?"

"Sorely tempted, but there is something I need to do before the next body turns up."

Calderwood raised his eyebrows. "Anything I can help with?"

McCord shook his head. "I'm going to create a file detailing all of Struthers' cock-ups. The list is pretty impressive already. And if he ever tries to suck up to Hepburn again by denouncing my team, I won't rest until he's been transferred to the Outer Hebrides, I swear."

* * *

McCord was about to go home to catch up on much needed sleep when he got a call from Hepburn to come and see him.

Muttering a curse, he rose. He felt too tired to fend off another tsunami of support and appreciation, but it had to be done.

When he knocked on the door, he heard a strange duet of "Come in!"

Inside the office, he was greeted warmly by Hepburn, who was looking bereft. Next to her, with a sombre expression on his pale face, stood Superintendent Arthur Gilchrist. To mark the occasion, he had donned his uniform, and stood as tall as he could possibly manage, dwarfing both Hepburn and McCord.

"Good evening, DI McCord," Gilchrist boomed. "I thought it fitting for you to thank DCI Hepburn on behalf of the station for the sterling job she has done during my absence. We've just got word that she is needed back at Gayfield Square."

"Oh, ah, alright," McCord stammered, completely taken by surprise. "Thank you, ma'am. It was good working with you."

They shook hands, Hepburn holding his gaze a few seconds longer than necessary. "It was a privilege, Russell," she said. "Maybe our paths will cross again some day."

McCord nodded, fervently hoping they would not.

Hepburn picked up the cardboard box with her personal belongings and, head held high, exited through the door that Gilchrist gallantly had opened for her.

When she had gone, Gilchrist sat down on his leather armchair with a sigh of pleasure.

"I take it you are feeling better, sir?" McCord asked.

"As good as new," Gilchrist said. "Thanks to our marvellous NHS, my stomach lining has been repaired."

He regarded McCord with his usual mixture of despair and enforced patience. "I gather that in the meantime you have finally managed to arrest a serial killer who had been running rings round you for the past few months. Ach, well, better late than never, eh, McCord?"

Gilchrist's countenance, however, changed to confusion, laced with suspicion, when McCord smiled.

"It's good to have you back, sir."

List of characters

Police

Detective Inspector Russell McCord
Detective Sergeant Duncan Calderwood
Superintendent Arthur Gilchrist
Detective Chief Inspector Audrey Hepburn
Detective Sergeant Walter Struthers
Detective Constable Heather 'The Hacker' Sutton
PC Surina Dharwan
PC Mike Turner
Jack Carruthers – Duty Sergeant
Dr Cyril Crane – pathologist

Amy Thornton's circle

Amy Thornton – journalist with *Forth Write* magazine
Martin Eden – subeditor of *Forth Write* magazine
John Campbell – owner of *Forth Write* magazine
Valerie Thornton – Amy's mother and partner of John

Others

Jai Sandhu – shopkeeper murdered in Edinburgh
Sarah Cartwright – victim
Ross Cartwright – husband of Sarah Cartwright
Amanda (Mandy) Jackson – friend of Sarah Cartwright
Daniel Slater – lottery winner

Yvonne Dunbar – Daniel Slater's girlfriend
Kimberley MacLean – former lover of Daniel Slater
Riley MacLean – Kimberley's infant son
Richard McAllister – half-brother of Daniel Slater
Karen McAllister – adoptive mother of Richard McAllister
Gordon McPhail – lottery winner
Giovanni – waiter at Mamma Roma
Graham Knight – social worker
Darren Pollock – Hibernian FC supporter
Dylan – bartender at Freddy's
Keith McCord – DI McCord's father
Clare Hildreth – McCord's father's fiancée

If you enjoyed this book, please let others know by leaving a quick review on Amazon. Also, if you spot anything untoward in the paperback, get in touch. We strive for the best quality and appreciate reader feedback.

editor@thebookfolks.com

Also in this series

NEAR MISS (book 1)

After being nearly hit by a car, fashion journalist Amy Thornton decides to visit the driver, who ends up in hospital after evading her. Curious about this strange man she becomes convinced she's unveiled a murder plot. But it won't be so easy to persuade Scottish detective DI Russell McCord.

HIGH HAND (book 2)

When a man is killed after a shooting party on a Scottish
country estate, DI McCord gets nowhere interviewing the
arrogant landowners. He'll have to rely on information passed
on by journalist Amy Thornton, who is more accustomed to
high society. But will his class resentment colour his
judgement when it comes to putting the murderer behind
bars?

LAST TRAIN FOR MURDER (book 3)

An investigative journalist who made a career out of sticking it to the man dies on a train to Edinburgh, having been poisoned. DI Russell McCord struggles in the investigation after getting banned from contacting helpful but self-serving reporter Amy Thornton. But the latter is ready to go in, all guns blazing. After the smoke has cleared, what will remain standing?

SHIFTING ICE (book 4)

After a jewellery thief meets a bitter end, DI McCord tries to make sense of his dying words. Are they a clue to his killer? He'll find out. Meanwhile journalist Amy Thornton is forbidden from taking on dangerous investigations, and sent on a fool's errand. Hmmm. She'll wiggle out of just about anything. Except perhaps the place she might hold in the cop's heart.

BRIGHT SPARKS (book 5)

The death of a local businesswoman in a house fire has grumpy detective Russell McCord running around in circles looking for the culprit. Sassy journalist Amy Thornton has some ideas of her own. But when the smoke has cleared, can the two crime-solvers put their differences aside and their heads together to work out the truth?

PARTING WORDS (book 7)

When sassy Edinburgh journalist Amy Thornton infiltrates an
environmental activist group, little does she know that one of
its members, stalked by an ex-boyfriend, will soon be
murdered. Thus she will collide once again with bumbling
cop DI Russell McCord. Anyone would think it's their
destiny to be ever entwined, whether they like it or not!

*All FREE with Kindle Unlimited and available in paperback and
hardback from Amazon.*

Other titles of interest

THE CRIMSON HARVEST
by Cheryl Rees-Price

Unflappable cop DI Winter Meadows has his wedding plans
interrupted when bodies begin to turn up on his patch. The
Welsh police have a serial killer on their hands and no stone
is left unturned in the hunt. But only a detective who truly
understands the community will be able to catch a killer in
their midst.

TO CATCH A LIE
by John Dean

DCI Jack Harris's day off on the river is interrupted when a man's body is found. The detective suspects the murder is connected with animal rights activists' attacks on local anglers but it seems he's fishing with rotten bait. The investigation takes him to Scotland, and out on a limb with regards to the opinions of his team.

*Sign up to our mailing list to find out about new releases
and special offers!*

www.thebookfolks.com

www.ingramcontent.com/pod-product-compliance
Lightning Source LLC
Chambersburg PA
CBHW030931210726
48290CB00007B/2157